THE
NIGHTMARE
CHRYSALIS

THE
NIGHTMARE
CHRYSALIS

A Novel of Suspense

Rosemary Gatenby

DODD, MEAD & COMPANY/*New York*

1 2 3 4 5 6 7 8 9 10

Library of Congress Cataloging in Publication Data

Gatenby, Rosemary.
    The nightmare chrysalis.

    I. Title.
PZ4.G26Ni [PS3557.A86]   813'.5'4   77–21531
ISBN 0–396–07490–1

For Bill

1972537

PROLOGUE

In just that moment when he put his hands on her, he had changed. A thrill of fear like a low electric current had gone through her.

Everything she knew about him—as with sudden, unwelcome insight she looked back upon it—twisted itself now into a different shape and told her he was dangerous.

But that was impossible unless he were other than what everyone believed him to be.

It had been for only a matter of seconds that he grasped her; in that short a time his intentions had been communicated. She'd broken away, in the starlit darkness, and had run.

Her legs trembled—from fear and exertion. And they stung where she'd scratched them running through a patch of nettles.

She stood in the shelter of the woods, her chest heaving.

Her heart pounded. She leaned against a tree trunk and tried to stop the rasping of her breath. She listened, but she could make out no sound of his pursuit; all she could hear was the deep-toned barking of the dog, Monty, who was shut in the house.

Light seeped through the trees from the carriage lamps on either side of Ferguson Brady's front door. She could see the dark outline of the Victorian doghouse against the porch.

Was she, too, silhouetted against the lighted house?

She crouched low and readied herself for a dash. If only she could make it . . .

Her skin crawled; she almost whimpered aloud . . . There was heavy breathing not five feet away.

This can't be happening, she thought. In a little while I'll be home, and I'll be laughing at myself because I was dumb enough to think that . . .

Should she scream?

If only she was off the path, not right here where—

She heard the scuffing of his shoe against a rock, and then a stealthy footfall. She heard the sound of his body coming toward her.

But now she could not have screamed. It was as though she were paralyzed. The thought went through her head: either it'll happen or it won't. Either I'll be safe and home soon in bed . . . or I won't.

She willed him to pass her by, unseeing, in the dark of the woods.

But he stopped beside her, and before she could scream, his hand was clamped over her mouth.

2

ONE

"A genuine recluse," Donna Church explained to Alice Jenner the May morning that Alice arrived back in Chillingworth after an absence of six years.

Alice had driven up from New York and had come straight to the real estate agency to pick up her key—Chillingworth Realty having had the rental of the Jenner house in its charge ever since the family had left Connecticut. Finding Donna behind one of the desks in the office had been a surprise.

"I didn't know you worked here!" she'd said; but then how would she have known—she'd lost touch with old friends after she'd moved away.

Donna had scarcely changed since they'd been in school together. She still wore her blonde hair hanging long down her back, still laughed with high-pitched exuberance, tilting her face up so that the gold loops dangling from her pierced ears swung like pendulums.

"But really, Donna, you mean Ferguson is—"

"Oh, he hikes down to the grocery and back—" The gold loops oscillated as she nodded in the direction of Smithfield's

Market a little to the north, and the hill on which Ferguson Brady lived, up that way. "And he's got a ten-speed bike. I see him go by on it once in a while."

"He still doesn't drive a car?"

"No. He sold his mother's when she passed away. Hasn't got one."

"But he's so young to be . . ." Alice hesitated, not ready to brand with some uncomplimentary word the boy she had once known.

"So eccentric?" Donna supplied.

"Oh," said Alice impulsively, "he can't be *really* eccentric! Just a little withdrawn?"

"Call it what you want to, he's certainly not like anybody *else* in town. . . ."

Alice went down the steps of the old Cape Cod house that had been made into an office and, frowning, got into her car. She had looked forward to seeing him again—had wondered whether he still lived here. She would have been disappointed, she realized, to learn that he was married. But to hear that he was so out of sync with life as it is generally lived . . .

She'd go and see him as soon as she had her more pressing problems under control. Right now there wasn't even any running water in the house, she'd been told—something wrong with the pump. And the phone wasn't connected yet . . .

Alice headed home. A nice sound to it, she thought, when once again it meant the old family homestead weathering in the spring sunshine in its setting among the oaks and maples above the river—and not a high-rise apartment to be shacked up in with a man you probably wouldn't marry even if he asked you.

TWO

Chillingworth, Connecticut, is a little north and east of Wilton, a little south of Danbury. It's a stop, actually, on the Danbury line of the railroad—though with only two trains in the morning and two in the evening. Because of this limited schedule, the number of residents who commute from the Chillingworth station to New York City is naturally small; most people drive to work—to jobs in White Plains, Stamford, Danbury. There is little employment available in Chillingworth, because no industrial plants are allowed within its borders.

Chillingworth doesn't look like a town at all; being zoned for two-acre building lots, it's pretty much spread out. And there are no sidewalks. There are a drugstore and a grocery in two old buildings across the tracks from the station. Over on the highway to Danbury that cuts through town there's the school—a jumble of low shapes in dark brick looking as if they're still waiting to be assembled into a recognizable structure—and across the road from it, neoclassical in style, the town hall, which has a bunch of offices at the rear, in the basement, for the police department.

Next to the town hall is the fire station. Its three engines are manned, when needed, by volunteers. And down the highway is a Chevron station; past that the Congregational church, with its white New England spire. The Catholic church, St. Anthony's, is up the other way a couple of miles to the north of town. And although the miles-long Chillingworth Reservoir, nestled between high, forested hills, provides a touch of beauty to the area, the water it contains is destined for one of the cities to the south of it, down on Long Island Sound; Chillingworth makes do with wells—and of course septic tanks—which contribute to its unspoiled rural charm.

There are the natives in Chillingworth, and there are the new people. Some of the new people have been residents for more than forty years and think of themselves as natives, but they're mistaken. To qualify as a Chillingworthian, your family must have owned land within the town borders well before 1900—preferably before 1800. The term "Johnny-come-lately" could well have been coined here. For instance, J. D. Pelsit, president of a big company in Danbury, is a nobody compared to his next-door neighbor, Fennimore Swanzey, who runs an apple and cider stand on the highway, purveying fruit from acres planted and tended by Swanzeys since 1723.

There were always Fergusons in Chillingworth—until the last of them, Gladys, married a man named Brady, from Waterbury, and brought him home as a groom to live in the old Ferguson house. No one ever heard much from Herbert Brady. He was an accountant, and over a period of years he held a series of jobs in different places, to which he drove five days a week. He fathered a son. But the consensus was that Gladys was just too much for Herbert. He withered away, blighted perhaps by the robustness of her personality, and

6

after only a few years in her care no longer had the strength to work. For a time he puttered about the house, and sometimes he helped out in the Antique Barn she ran. But eventually he shrivelled up and died, when his son, Ferguson Clarence, was still only a small boy.

Herbert Brady had been a nice-looking man before he had shrivelled, and his son grew up physically to resemble him —nice-looking, with light brown hair, blue eyes, and a nose that was irregular in shape and a little too long. He had an easy smile and broad shoulders, but when fully grown was not quite as tall as his mother, who was an even six feet without shoes and weighed somewhat over two hundred pounds.

Gladys Brady died of a cerebral hemorrhage when Ferguson was twenty-eight years old. Fergie thereupon retired from his job at the bank in New York City to which he had commuted and became a full-time recluse—not because his mother's death had been any sort of crushing blow, or because he was beginning to wither like his father before him, but because he hated banking.

Those first weeks—months actually—alone in the house had been heaven. Never having tried to visualize the place without his mother, he was amazed at how pleasant it was now that she was gone.

He had grieved when she died, certainly—though more for her sake than for his own. He knew how bitterly she would have resented being cut down at the age of sixty-two, if she had known about it. And he had loved his mother—or thought he had. The strange thing was that he didn't miss her or long for her return after the funeral. His affection for her seemed larger and warmer now than it ever had before —it was a thing perfect in itself, complete; he could almost hold it in his hand. Though he didn't realize the reason for this feeling of his, which was the absence of the quotidian irritations and annoyances that had made up their life. Anyone who had known Gladys Brady either well or slightly could have told him that she had always been one of those people whom absence makes the heart grow fonder of because in person they drive you up the wall. No one told him this, naturally. It is much easier to speak well of the dead and ill of the living.

And so he supposed that the reason he wasn't more bowed down with grief was that he was in shock—the fact that she was dead simply hadn't come home to him yet. And in the meantime it was as though he were on an extended vacation.

It was possible now, while he was watching old Bogart movies, to put his feet up on the footstool that matched the easy chair before the television set in the music room. He could eat as early or late as he chose and as unbalanced a meal as he liked—canned baked beans and half an apple pie or steak and ice cream. He could leave his shoes by the door and live barefoot in the house. At last Monty could come inside, instead of wintering in his Victorian doghouse in the side yard and summering on the front porch.

Fergie sold off everything in the Antique Barn, down at the edge of his property on the highway, and brought up to the house from down there, the cat, Mitzi, whom his mother had had declawed to spare the furniture while Mitzi kept mice out of the upholstery.

But he had not foreseen how solitary his life was going to be.

A lot of things went back, didn't they, to that November night when he'd been only nineteen: it had divided his life into two parts, before and after. Because he had no friends. Not now. Not here.

Acquaintances—sure. Older people, middle-aged, around

town. But nobody his age to be friends with. You made friends when you were a kid in school. Again at college—and he'd had friends at college, but they were scattered now. Ostensibly you made friends where you worked. But the kind of people who went into banking didn't seem to be his sort. Now that he wasn't even in the bank . . . And so four years had passed.

It was on a Saturday in May that Fergie's life at last took a change in direction. It was the same day—had he but known it—that Alice Jenner and the young man with whom she had cohabited for the last eighteen months quarreled violently and Alice decided upon a return to the town where she had grown up—for which she had cherished fond and nostalgic feelings for at least two years now without understanding why, because she had hated the place when she lived there.

Fergie's decision on that Saturday morning didn't seem like much when he made it, but the eventual effects were far-reaching. All he decided, really, was to walk down the hill to the barn that had formerly been his mother's antique shop to see what they'd done with the place now that it had been converted into a theater.

He had been filling out a questionnaire—a survey of some kind from the university he had attended. He had happily put down all sorts of information about himself . . . NAME: *Ferguson Clarence Brady.* ADDRESS: *8 Hill Road, Chillingworth, Connecticut.* AGE: *32.* DEGREES: *B.A.* UNDERGRADUATE MAJOR: *English Literature.* GRADUATE STUDIES: *None.* MARITAL STATUS: *Single.* CHILDREN: *None.* GRANDCHILDREN: *None.* INCOME?

He checked the box *$15,000–$20,000*—that was roughly

what his mother's investments brought in.

OCCUPATION?

He was always hung up over that question. None? Retired? Ex-banker? Woodworker? Furniture maker? . . .

Suddenly he found himself wondering why he was so happy racking his brain for answers to put down—as though someone, somewhere, were really interested in what he was like, what he had done. As though that someone cared . . . Why? Who did he think was interested; who cared? The deviser of the form? The tabulator of the results? My God, he thought, I'm so desperate for a little companionship I'm ready to cosy up to some computer—if only it'll listen to me . . .

He dropped the questionnaire into the wastebasket.

"Monty!" he called to the great, gaunt Irish wolfhound. "Let's go for a walk."

They went down the steps of the big mustard-colored Victorian house with its square tower topped by iron cresting and took the path through the woods, the one that went downhill toward the barn.

"We'll go and see what they've done with it," Fergie said to his companion, who was well used to confidences of this sort. When he'd sold the barn and four acres to go with it, a step necessitated months ago by inflation and the tax rise caused by the building of the new school, he'd supposed the purchaser would convert it into a house—there were plenty of houses made out of barns in this part of Connecticut. When he'd learned of the theater project, he hadn't known whether to be intrigued or appalled.

The path was the shortcut that his mother used to take. It wound through the trees, some of it over stones green with lichen, some of it over ground where no grass or weeds grew because of the dense shade, where moss and ground pine

10

covered the earth. The path was still used by Monty and, no doubt, by the wild inhabitants of the area as well—skunk, possum, raccoon, and an occasional deer.

Along the far edge of the woods was a stone fence; beyond it a large field. Where the path and the fence intersected, the stones were tumbled down and scattered. It was from here he had watched the activity on the other side of the field as they worked at converting the barn—watched, resting one foot on the stone fence, a wall made over two hundred years ago by John Ferguson and his sons, using the stones prized out of the field, stones rounded by glacial action and deposited there at the end of the last ice age. Fergie had watched the lumber being delivered for construction of the interior, listened to the shriek of the power saw and to the sound of the hammering, watched while eager helpers slapped red barn stain all over the outside and freshened up the trim with new white.

It was to be an amateur theater—local talent. Some of the same talent who hoped to be on the stage were the ones doing the painting—so he had read in the paper. Frank Wells had of course kept him up-to-date, too, on the project. Frank was a long-time dabbler in amateur theatricals.

Fergie and Monty crossed the field, where the path became less distinct. The grass grew high every summer, rife with daisies, black-eyed Susans, Queen Anne's lace, and goldenrod, but now it was still flattened—beaten down by the weight of the winter's snow and the ice, and by the winds that had blown across it when the old grass was soggy with rain.

Fergie squeezed between a pair of rails of the two-rail fence surrounding the parking lot, in which stood several cars.

The old back door through which he'd entered for years was still there, but no telling where it led. He wouldn't want to go in that way. Along the side was a series of three double doors, all new, all closed—exits decreed by Chief Pennywith, the fire chief, no doubt. Fergie went around to the front.

A sign lettered in old-style script CHILLINGWORTH LITTLE THEATRE, black on a white oval, swung between two posts sunk in the earth by the entrance from the highway.

What had been a display window in his mother's day was now a wide door, the main way into the theater. Through it drifted the sound of voices reading lines.

"Stay," he said to Monty and went in.

He was in the theater lobby. On his left was a counter for the sale of tickets, and on the right a wall with two posters —both the same, advertising *Golden Boy* as the first production of the company. The walls were of unstained knotty pine.

He walked through an open door into the theater.

"No, not *that* way! Your hands. Your hands are what is important here—they're a violinist's hands." A mid-Atlantic accent; it was neither American nor English—just stagey. The voice belonged to a tall, broad-shouldered man with a slight stoop, who stood in the aisle addressing the little group of actors on the bare stage. Fergie recognized him as Christopher Durham, one of the new people in town whose name and picture appeared frequently in the pages of *The Chillingworth Chronicle.* Professor Durham was head of the drama department at Dumont College up north of Danbury.

The rehearsal resumed. Fergie, leaning against the wall at the back, found himself unexpectedly skewered by a shaft of emotion straight from the past, as the young lead, the one who was "the golden boy," began to speak. The actor was so like Chad had been—the set of the face, with the wide-spaced Slavic cheekbones; the full-lipped mouth; the mop of dark wavy hair.

12

In a long sigh, Fergie let out the breath he must have been holding. The face up there belonged to someone whose name he didn't even know. But for a minute the resemblance had turned the clock back thirteen years. He saw again the headlights rushing toward them in the blackness, saw their reflection on wet pavement, heard the sound of the crash and the terrible silence afterward.

He put the scene out of his mind for perhaps the millionth time and took a seat in the last row.

Benches with backs had been put in for seats—like bleachers. Everything had been done as simply as possible. No proscenium, no curtain. The stage jutted out into the first rows of benches, which were angled on either side to accommodate it.

Two girls sat on the edge of the apron, watching. He guessed they were members of the cast—one black-haired, Italianate, the other a lively, pretty blonde with a model's face. He had once seen the blonde getting into her car in front of the grocery, and another time she'd been on the train when he'd taken it into New York—not a face or figure you'd be likely to forget.

The only one he actually knew of the people onstage was Frank Wells, who was married to Fergie's cousin Leona. Leona Franklin she'd been. Her grandmother had been a Ferguson; her mother and his had been first cousins.

And Frank owned the drugstore in Chillingworth.

Since his mother's death, Fergie saw very little of Leona; the visiting back and forth that had once gone on had stopped. Thanksgiving dinner at her house was obligatory, because she wouldn't hear of his sitting down to a solitary dinner on that day. Otherwise he generally succeeded in avoiding Leona. She was nice enough—cloying, in fact. Like most women.

13

He found the air of domesticity at the Wells house stifling. Leona's passion for ruffles—on lampshades, on pillows, on slipcovers—and for cutesy items of decor—cuckoo clocks, pink china poodles with gilt bangs, sentimentalized pictures of kittens and of huge-eyed "darling" waifs in shadow-box frames—made her living room a nightmare to sit in. Add to all that boudoir fussiness the Wells children, horrors all three—oh, the oldest one was all right now, a girl in high school—

Frank had the part of the young boxer's father, Mr. Bonaparte. He was pretty good, Fergie discovered. Surprising. He wouldn't have expected anyone with Frank's lack of flair to have a gift for the drama. Proving that you never could judge by appearances, even when you'd known someone moderately well for over twenty years.

The scene came to an end.

"I see we have our first critic." Durham had turned and was facing the rear of the theater, causing Fergie to become immediately the focus of all eyes.

He wished that he had not come.

"Hi, Ferguson!" Frank called out.

Long ago his friends had called him Fergie. Now that he had no friends he was "Ferguson" or "Mr. Brady." The nickname was lost, with so much else.

Christopher Durham strode up the aisle to stand beside him—a man of about his own age, Fergie observed, with an aggressive manner, and an acquisitive glint in his somewhat close-set hazel eyes.

"You must be Ferguson Brady. I'm Chris Durham."

Fergie got to his feet. "How do you do." He put out his hand and it was nearly crushed in the other's grasp.

"I've been wanting to meet you. We need some help with

14

our sets, you see, and I understand you know a lot about furniture?"

Frank had jumped down from the stage and followed the director up the aisle. He stood at Durham's elbow, looking ill at ease.

"You even have a woodworking shop at your place, I hear?" the mid-Atlantic voice pursued.

"Well, yes, I do have . . . I turn out a few reproductions of old—"

"We could use you. And your shop."

Fergie stood frozen. This person wanted to intrude himself into his shop in the old carriage house and nail flats together?

"Well, I certainly don't—" He broke off, appalled at the mere idea of anyone else handling his saws and planes.

Frank smiled an apology. "I'm sorry, Ferguson. I started this."

Another of Frank's efforts to do his wife's cousin a kindness. He and Leona had tried repeatedly, right after Gladys had died, to pry him out of his solitude. Fergie had thought they'd given up by now.

Frank turned to Durham. "I didn't mean to suggest we use his shop. Anyhow Gene's got the construction end of things pretty much worked out. I thought Ferguson might help out in an advisory capacity, that's all."

"Or lend us a saw now and then?" Durham smiled placatingly.

"I'm sorry, but—"

"Ferguson, don't say no right off." Frank smiled at him with the shy, homely smile familiar to Fergie from twenty years of seeing it on the other side of the drugstore counter. "What I had in mind when I mentioned you to Chris was that maybe you could recruit furniture for us. Because of

your mother's shop you must know a bunch of antique dealers around here. Some of them might be glad to lend us stuff.
It would mean a free advertisement for them in the program."

"Exactly," Durham agreed, patting Fergie on the arm.
"Isn't that what I said we'd like you to do for us?" No, it
hadn't been.

"I suppose I could," Fergie hesitantly admitted.

"Good." Chris Durham gave him no time to quibble.
"That's settled, then. You'll be working with Gene Mack—
he's in charge of sets. You know him, I imagine?"

Fergie didn't, but then he knew very few of the new people
in town.

Taking Ferguson by the arm, Durham led him down front
and introduced him to everyone who was on hand. The
blonde, whose name was Marta Guild; the black-haired girl,
Lucy Cannon. Ed Skinner, who played the fight manager.
Ralph somebody; someone named Smith; a clutch of girls
giggling in the front row.

The young lead who looked so much like Chad was a boy
named Malcolm Ludlow. Close up the resemblance was still
uncanny.

The company went on with the next scene, but Fergie had
had enough. He left them and went out into the sunlight.
Monty got up, with a wag of his tail, from where he'd been
lying next to the old bench beside the open double doors—
the same bench that used to be by the door around at the
rear. He and Alice Jenner used to sit there in the sun, their
backs against the warm, porous boards of the barn's west
wall, and talk.

That went back a long way—those two summers that
Alice had worked for his mother. She'd been only fourteen
the first summer. He remembered that because she couldn't

16

get a work permit until she was sixteen. "We'll just pay her sitter's fees," his mother had said. "She can sit with the furniture."

He was thinking about Alice as he and Monty crossed the field and started up through the woods. Alice was the only girl in Chillingworth with whom he'd ever felt at ease. The only girl anywhere, really, with whom he'd gotten along. Not just because she was younger—seven years younger, because he'd been twenty-one that summer. No, it hadn't been her age, because Alice had seemed older than she was—conversationally, anyway. What he'd always liked about Alice was that she was sincere, Alice was—not coy.

Well, she'd had nothing to be coy about, had she, with her sloppy looks—hair like a bird's nest, done up on top of her head, with wisps hanging down; round, dumpling-plain face; shapeless figure, obscured beneath the layers of dismal, shabby blouses, vests, sweaters, and tunics she wore whether the weather was hot or cold.

Even when she'd gotten older and he'd seen her around town she'd never had a boyfriend. Maybe that was why she was so straightforward, so bearable for a girl—she hadn't been always on the make.

As he came out of the woods into his yard, he was wondering what had ever become of Alice Jenner. Mr. Jenner had been transferred by his company to someplace in New York State, and the family had left when Alice was nineteen or twenty—while she'd still been at Vassar. He'd heard that she had graduated with honors.

"I'm too smart for my own good," she'd told him once. "Excess intelligence only makes you neurotic."

Fergie had never wondered whether he was neurotic or not.

*   *   *

Midafternoon when he heard a car in the drive he came out of his workshop.

There were two cars, parked one behind the other where the drive curved past the house. Chris Durham got out of the first and, catching sight of Ferguson, came striding toward him. Malcolm Ludlow and a girl, the occupants of the other car, followed desultorily in Durham's wake, talking to one another.

The drama professor carried two slender scrolls of paper, each secured by a rubber band.

"I've got the sketches of the sets here for the first two productions. We don't need much for *Golden Boy*—a park bench, a locker-room bench, some cheap, crummy chairs. The main things are a beat-up couch for the fight manager's office—we can cover it with a throw for the scenes in the Bonaparte home—and a long, sort of table-type desk. It's got to look like a desk, but with a cloth on it it'll be a dining-room table, and in the dressing-room scenes, at the boxing arena, it'll have to be a rubbing table. When we don't have a curtain to come down between scenes, you know . . ."

"Yes," Fergie said. "You've had to make the set changes as simple as possible."

"Right. And that's part of the fun."

"What's your second play going to be?"

"*Blithe Spirit.* It's on that one where we'll really need your talents—and your connections. An English country drawing room. We've got to have good stuff. But I'll show you later what—" He broke off. "That your workshop?" He nodded toward the carriage house.

"Yes," Fergie said rather stiffly. He saw no reason for his visitors even to set foot in there.

"Could we have a look? Oh"—as the others caught up

18

with him—"you already know Malcolm, and this is Maryellen Polk."

"Maryellen spelled together in one word," the girl spe-
cified, perhaps trying to nail down her identity with the
spelling of her name.

She was a very pretty girl, Fergie saw, with the burgeoning
beauty of feature she shared with thousands of other girls
whose faces had not yet set into the mold of maturity. She
had the short upper lip that can be so appealing, translucent
blue eyes, and hair of a dark honey color shot with red
highlights that might be natural and might be the result of
a rinse.

"Gene Mack's not available today—he's on duty," Durham explained. "We'll have to go over this without him. But
I brought Maryellen along. She's chief set painter."

"He just calls me that so I'll work harder." Maryellen
smiled, showing her milk-white teeth.

"I designed the sets, but Gene's in charge of construction.
You said you know Gene?"

"No."

Durham gestured with the rolled drawings. "On the Chillingworth police force." The gesture had been meant, apparently, to indicate the town hall.

"Oh." The Chillingworth Police Department was about a
year old. Prior to its inception, the town had had only a
resident state trooper and some deputies. Fergie had seen the
new police cars—sky blue and white—and had passed one or
another of the officers going into or out of the drugstore, but
he had met none of them personally.

"Officer Mack's in charge of sets, and I'm in charge of
furniture?" he asked.

"Roughly. That's about it. Could we see your . . .?"

Reluctantly—this visit to his shop was an invasion of his privacy—Fergie took them into the light and airy interior of the sturdy mustard-yellow building with the cupola topped by the running-horse weather vane.

He stood at the front of the old carriage house and from there pointed out his workbench in the right rear corner, under the windows—the extra ones he had put in along the side and the back so that he'd have good daylight for his work.

"Nothing much to see," he said.

But the little group, looking small for the height of the place, edged on into the far end of the room. The afternoon sunlight slanted far above their heads from the round window high in the west wall.

The girl looked about, her eyes passing over the tack board with its saws and hammers, the racks and stands with his carving tools. She was not interested—just filling time, waiting.

"Great bench saw you have here." The drama professor reached out a hand. Fergie was afraid Durham was about to touch it, but he didn't.

Only the boy, Malcolm, was really interested in the shop, in what he was doing here. Fergie could tell by the way he studied the rows of tools—the rifflers, the gouges—although he said nothing.

Fergie felt drawn to the boy because of his resemblance to Chad. But when Malcolm Ludlow happened suddenly to meet his gaze, he was embarrassed and looked away.

His glance landed instead on Maryellen.

Her fingers were twined through Malcolm's, and she stood beside him doing nothing at all, her lips slightly parted. Exuding sexuality. Unconsciously? Or was it something she did on purpose?

"A nice boy isn't safe with a girl like that," his mother would have said.

Well, Maryellen was Malcolm Ludlow's affair—not his.

But she made him uncomfortable. Girls always did, especially the pretty ones.

When the little group had gone—after he'd looked at the drawings of the sets and made mental note of what would be needed—he was relieved. He was glad to be rid of them. Yet he found that he was curiously excited by this new prospect before him. He was looking forward to being a part of this little bit of the theater world that had taken up residence at the bottom of his hill.

At the same time, the thought of working with Maryellen nagged at him. What had he gotten himself into?

THREE

Alice removed the grime from the windows, stripped off the peeling wallpaper in the downstairs bathroom, and washed down the walls that were scarred and marred by the succession of renters that had occupied the house. She found herself occasionally wondering whether she had taken a step forward or a step back in coming here? Was she retreating from her new, hard-won individuality? Regressing psychologically?

She didn't know.

On Monday afternoon the pump man had come—the same one who had tended it whenever it was ailing in the years her mother and dad had lived here. Water had been restored and once more gushed from the faucets.

Tuesday she cleaned all day. Wednesday more of the same. She thought of going over to see Ferguson Brady but decided that first she'd better finish what she was doing.

She was still working on Wednesday evening, with all the ceiling fixtures turned on because she had no lamps as yet, when the hollow sound of the brass door knocker being dropped reverberated through the empty rooms of the house.

With one arm—because her hands were wet—she pushed the short, dark hair back from her face, then with slippery fingers managed to get the front door open.

A tall man with a self-confident slouch, carefully groomed curly hair, and a small mustache lounged on the stoop.

"I'm your neighbor," he said. "Chris Durham." His appraising glance, starting at her ankles and traveling upward, warned her to be wary of this one.

"Hello. You live next door?"

"No. End of the road. Three houses farther on. I was driving by when I saw your lights."

And stopped his car and came and peered in the curtainless windows at her, no doubt?

He straightened a little from his slouch, preparatory to entering. "Welcome to Chillingworth." A male chauvinist smile spread over his face.

"Thanks. You haven't lived here too long yourself, have you?"

He looked slightly and genially puzzled. "Three-four years . . ."

"I'm Alice Jenner. This is my family's house."

"Jenner. Oh, yes—the people who just moved out were renting, weren't they. Alice? Welcome back, Alice! May I come in?"

"Oh, sure." She moved aside and he stepped into the hall, making its low ceiling look lower. The Jenner house was an old one, built in the seventeen hundreds when people were smaller and when spaciousness caused a heating problem.

"Your family moving in again?"

"No, just me."

He walked into the living room, where he glanced around at the stepladder, pail of suds, broom, and mop. The room was good-sized, a result of two rooms having been made into

23

one. "You're doing all this by yourself?"

"Why not?"

"You better let me come over and lend a hand."

She smiled guardedly. "Thanks. If I run into something too heavy to handle . . ."

"Right now I think what you need is to knock off and come over to my place for a drink."

"Sounds like a nice idea. Some other time."

"No, really."

"I couldn't. If I sat down with a drink, I wouldn't be able to get up again. Besides, I'm hardly dressed for cocktails." She indicated with a gesture the dirty rolled-up jeans and stained tee shirt that were her working uniform.

"Oh, you look *fine!*" She guessed that what he really meant was that braless, she met with his hearty approval. She regretted not wearing a loose-fitting shirt.

"Well, thanks, but I plan to just collapse here at home." She moved slowly but definitely toward the front hall. "Nice of you to stop in . . ."

"Dinner?" he inquired, trailing reluctantly after her to the door. "I've got every kind of TV dinner you might want— chicken, swiss steak, chinese, sauerbraten . . ."

"No, thanks." She had reached the door and she opened it.

"I wish you *would* come. I'm all alone."

"That's more of a deterrent that an inducement. I gather you're not usually alone?"

"*Now* I am. My wife's gone. Took the kids."

"Then you'll just have to manage till she gets back."

He shook his head. "Isn't coming back. Or so she says."

"My condolences, then—if that's what's in order. Or maybe she'll change her mind."

He stood on the threshold.

24

"Call me the minute you need some help—moving in, spading up the garden, mending screens. Anything. Okay?"

"Right. I appreciate the offer."

"See you, then."

Probably, she thought as she closed the door. End of the road. He passed her house every time he went anywhere—or came back.

But she didn't want to become involved, even tangentially, in his domestic tangle, whatever it was.

Fergie and Officer Gene Mack failed, from their very first meeting, to hit it off.

Officer Mack had squiggly eyebrows, like bad handwriting. They drew easily into a frown and as easily into a quizzical expression. It was not his fault, of course, that they enabled him to look both displeased and enquiring at the same time—handy, perhaps, during interrogations conducted on the job. His chin was round, with a dimple in it, and his teeth were too small for his face—and being small, when he smiled there seemed to be an unnaturally large number of them.

But his smile was not very friendly. At least Fergie didn't think so.

Mack showed up on Monday morning, when Fergie was in his shop working. Announced by some barking from Monty, he walked in, introduced himself, and looked around.

A dark-complexioned face, a dark head of hair—straight, with one lock falling over the forehead. A conceited face, Fergie thought. He saw on it a grudging respect for the tools of Fergie's craft and for the partially finished furniture that stood around, but antagonism for the owner of the place.

He wondered, why the antagonism?

25

"You live in Chillingworth?" he asked the policeman, trying to inject a personal note into their meeting.

"No. Up near Danbury."

Dumb question, Fergie realized too late. On his policeman's salary, Mack could not afford a house in Chillingworth. A few small homes that predated the zoning laws existed here and there around town, but with the two-acre zoning, the price of land, and the demand by commuters to live in this kind of community, the price of a house in Chillingworth had skyrocketed.

"I understand," his visitor went on rather sourly, "that you're some kind of authority on furniture."

"Not exactly. I fuss around with it some, as you can see."

"Chris and I have already worked out the sets, you know. There won't be much for you to do—not on the first two plays, anyhow."

(*Chris and I,* huh? Durham had credited himself with the design of the sets; Mack was only mentioned as being on the construction end.)

"That's fine with me. I'm not too sure what I *am* supposed to be doing . . ."

"Advising. That's how it was told to me."

And Officer Mack didn't want anyone advising him, that was clear. He wanted to be unequivocally in charge.

"Procuring—if you don't mind the term." Fergie said with a little smile. The man gave him a quick, perhaps startled glance. "Of the furniture. That's what I understood they wanted me for. I have a lot of contacts with antique dealers."

"Oh, yes." Didn't crack a smile. No sense of humor. "I guess that'll be a help."

"And you're in charge, I understand, of putting it all together."

26

"Yes, that's right."

Yet something still rankled. Perhaps it was the term *adviser.*

Fergie had just finished lunch on Thursday when the sharp ring of the doorbell—it was an electric bell, not chimes—announced a visitor.

One of the theater group, no doubt.

Monty was already en route to the front door from the kitchen.

Not one of the group with whom he was acquainted, Ferguson discovered, struck dumb by the beauty of the girl confronting him from the other side of the doormat on the front porch. Short dark hair curling softly about her face; lively brown eyes under delicately arched brows; cheekbones with those hollows under them, like Faye Dunaway or a fashion model . . . She was wearing gray slacks and a gray plaid shirt, which for some reason made her look more female than if she'd had on a dress.

"Yes?" he said. Girls like this threw him into a panic—he didn't know what to say to them. There they were, flaunting their charms at you, gazing up expectantly as though you were going to say something world-shaking, when actually your mind had gone blank and you felt like a freak calf with an extra leg.

"Gus . . ." she said. "You really don't recognize me?"

His surroundings seemed to change shape just a bit, and time stretched astigmatically in front of him, distorting what he saw. Only one person had ever called him Gus—("Well, it's part of your name, isn't it? Ferguson? Got a helluva lot more guts than 'Fergie.' ")

He passed his hand across his eyes, thinking something might change. It didn't. "You can't be! . . . Alice?"

He thought of the dumpling-faced girl with the bird's nest of hair, its tendrils trailing down the side of her neck; the girl with the shapeless figure swathed in layers of clothing . . .

Incredible.

So this was only Alice, after all.

She seemed gratified at his confusion.

He blinked one more time. "Well, if you say so . . ." He stepped backward, uncertainly, into the hall. "Come on in."

She took his hand as she stepped into the gloom of the house, and impulsively she laid the fingers of her other hand upon his wrist. From this sudden contact he discovered that she was not at all the girl Alice he had known long ago, a feckless child. This Alice was altogether different—grown— a woman.

He closed the door and trailed in after her.

"Still got your big dog, I see. He was a puppy when we moved away." Her hand rested on the dog's rough-coated head.

"Yes. Monty."

She stood in the middle of the old worn Karastan rug and looked around her.

Only three of the cats were in the living room, curled up on various chairs—Mitzi and two of the last litter she'd had before he'd gotten her fixed.

"Speak of an old maid and her cats . . ."

"That's Mitzi." He indicated the tortoise-shell one on the yellow velvet cushion.

"Oh, yes. She was down at the barn in the old days."

Alice put her hands on her hips. "Well, at least you haven't walled yourself in with stacks of old newspapers— or are they in another room?"

"What?" He had scarcely heard what she said, he was so busy adjusting to the new Alice.

28

"You're reputed locally to have become a recluse. I just wondered how far you'd gone in your chosen line of eccentricity. One hears . . ."

"Oh. Oh, yes . . ."

"But it's bad enough. Why don't you get rid of all this stuff?" She waved a hand at the contents of the room.

For probably the first time in his life Ferguson glanced about with an objective eye at the wall-to-wall clutter that was his living room. There were antiques of every period back to the sixteen hundreds, pieces his mother had prized plus the overflow from the shop. The Elizabethan chest; the Chippendale settee, its tapestry upholstery worn to tatters; the hideous late-Sheraton bookcase; the Hepplewhite inlaid work table; chairs lyre-backed, claw-footed, wreath-painted, satin-upholstered, rush-bottomed, caned, made of bentwood. The Art Deco firescreen; the Tiffany lamps; the windowsill-fulls of Bohemian glass; the breakfront stuffed with Meissen, Staffordshire, and unattributable horribilia. The untenanted Victorian bird cage.

"Well, I never use this room," he offered.

"Thank God for that, at least. But I'd think it would depress you just passing *through* here."

"I guess I'm immune. Anyhow I don't give it much thought."

"Come on, let's go in the kitchen. Can't we have a cup of coffee or something?" She flipped the fringe on the monstrous twenties floor lamp, causing it to undulate wildly. He followed her, with Monty, into the kitchen.

"It's your house, you know." She took over in the kitchen, and he watched her put the kettle on to heat, get out two mugs, and measure instant coffee into each. "Why don't you sell off ninety percent of that stuff and do the place the way you want it?" She looked around at him, where he'd seated himself at the hand-hewn colonial table his mother had acquired at a farm auction up in Vermont. "She's not coming back, you realize."

"Yes, I know. That's just it, I suppose. That in there"—he gestured in the direction of the living room—"is all that's left of her. Doesn't seem right to disturb it."

"A sort of earthly memorial? Oh, come on! For all the monstrosities your mother sold to customers over the years, she had more taste than is reflected in that living room. It was simply a warehouse from which she stocked the barn." He was listening, of course, but with attention divided, as the curve of her cheek, the thrust of her breasts under the plaid shirt, the roundness of her buttocks distracted him. This was Alice?

"You're sure the preserving of Gladys's treasures isn't simply your security blanket?"

He shook his head. "No. Bad conscience, maybe—because I never did anything to suit her. But you know that."

"So you're placating her shade."

"Goodness, no! I don't believe in immortality of any kind. When you're dead, you're gone completely. It's just never occurred to me to dispose of her things, that's all. They're hers, not mine."

"Well, you've got some kind of hang-up there. Everything that was hers is now yours. You're letting her dictate from beyond the grave . . . And I *was* very sorry, you know, to learn of her death. I enjoyed Gladys. Though it was much easier just to know her than to be related to her, I well realize."

He leaned back in his chair, with a small grin. "You're the only one who's said anything like that at all to me . . . since she died."

Alice poured water from the copper kettle, and steam rose

30

from the mugs. "Milk? Not for me . . ."

"Nor me."

As she sat down opposite him, he felt himself pierced by what seemed a ray of pure happiness. An old friend—here was an old friend with whom he could share recollections of times long gone.

He hadn't had an old friend to talk to in years.

"What are you doing here, Alice—passing through on your way somewhere?"

"No. I've come back to stay."

"To stay?"

There was a little line between her brows and a light tone of chagrin in her voice. "Well, don't say it like that! Can't you be a little happy about it?"

"I was just surprised. You used to hate Chillingworth."

"I had pitted myself against my environment then. Adolescent Alice. It's not the same set of circumstances now."

"Maybe you'll find you hate it in a different way."

"You're not very optimistic. Don't you like it here? If you don't, why do you stay?"

"Oh, it suits me fine."

"And you're going to stay here till you rot. The stacks of old newspapers eventually will—"

"So what are you going to do, when you've settled down here, that's so much better?"

"Get a job. Paralegal work again—that's what I've been doing down in New York. I can find a job in Stamford . . . or Danbury . . ."

"Um. Why did you leave New York? Didn't like it?"

She took a sip of her coffee before she answered. Then she carefully set down the mug. "I've been living with my boyfriend for the past year and a half. Lawyer—working for the same firm I was. Last week we reached what I could only see as a parting of the ways. He got custody of our employer, and I didn't want the apartment. My family's house here happened to be without a tenant at the moment, and that fact seemed providential. The decision to move out here practically made itself."

"Ah."

"Is that all you can say? 'Ah'? I don't know whether you're issuing condolences or a moral judgment—or what. I suppose I've just demonstrated for you that girls are as immoral and treacherous as your mother always told you they were."

He shrugged. "I've never tested out her theories." That wasn't exactly true, of course—Sharon had been—

"Or discarded them either, I gather."

"I don't bother particularly with any opinion about girls."

She sucked in her cheeks. "Well, the word *bother* sort of tells me where we stand."

"Oh, you're not to be lumped in with the others, Alice." He waved a hand in the air, dismissing the rest of the female sex. "You're different. We've always been friends."

"I used to be different, I guess. Am I still?"

"You mean are we still friends? Sure. You don't undo friendship. But you've changed—oh my!"

She looked at him consideringly. "I noticed that you'd noticed."

"You didn't merely grow up—it's more than that."

"Yes. I went into analysis. My whole concept of myself changed. I came out a different person."

"Oh."

"Don't sound so glum."

"Well, I was hoping you hadn't completely done away with the old Alice . . ."

"Thanks. That's some kind of a compliment, is it? Though

32

retroactive only, perhaps—no longer applicable? Oh, the old me is still at the core of things—somewhere."

But he doubted it from time to time, distrusting her when he looked at her—because of her changed appearance.

And yet he felt let down when she left. He put her into her shiny yellow Vega, and he and Monty watched her drive down to the road. They went back into the house, and despite all the clutter Alice had criticized, it seemed strangely empty.

FOUR

Ferguson's life had changed beyond all recognition. At first he felt like the outsider with his nose pressed against the pane, but soon he found himself inside, accepted as a full-fledged member of the theater group. It was amazing how a project of this sort could draw people together—it gave them something in common, something to talk about, a goal they all worked toward. Intimacies sprang up overnight in this world of make believe—and enmities.

Gene Mack, Fergie knew, thoroughly disliked him. And he himself as thoroughly disliked Chris Durham. The man was overbearing, conceited. Chris's every word, every action rubbed him the wrong way; but some of the fault, Fergie decided, must be with some oddball bias of his own, because everyone else adored the theater director. And the results Durham achieved were excellent. Clearly he was good at his job.

Which didn't mean Fergie had to like him.

It was strange how he continued to feel as if he'd known Malcolm all his life. Superficial as the resemblance to Chad might be, it was enough to give an illusion of familiarity to

34

everything Malcolm said and did. Whereas Fergie had for years shied away from any intimacy proferred by new people, within a matter of days he and the young lead in the *Golden Boy* production were fast friends.

There was an age gap, certainly—almost ten years—but Malcolm's interest in Fergie's woodworking shop made the difference inconsequential. Fergie had soon, in fact, taken him on as almost an apprentice, instructing him in the skills he had so lovingly acquired himself.

"I started out, you know, just doing a few repairs on the stuff my mother handled—gluing on a piece of trim that had fallen off or carving a replacement foot for an old chest. Then one of the customers at the barn wanted me to make a reproduction of a ladderback chair she had, to fill out her dining-room set. One thing led to another. Like this mirror frame I finally finished . . ."

"That's not old?"

1972537

"No. The original was lost in a fire. I worked from a photograph."

"But the wood looks old."

"It is. It's from a table top I found at the dump. I get a lot of my wood there. You wouldn't believe the things people throw out."

Yet what Malcolm most admired were the pieces of Fergie's own design. He had some time ago begun with the dining-room table—that was finished and in the house—and now was working on the chairs. This furniture was for him, not for a customer. The design was one that seemed to him to have a fluid grace—a motif of acanthus leaves, which he had used, not in a traditional way, but with a contemporary effect.

"It's beautiful," Malcolm said. "I've never seen anything like it."

Almost every afternoon when Malcolm finished work at the bank in Wilton—a coincidence that he had the same sort of job Fergie had once held—he came up to the workshop on the hill.

But with Malcolm came Maryellen. She was always hanging around. Although school in Connecticut ran into late June, little was expected of the seniors this close to commencement, so Maryellen had no homework.

She bothered Fergie until he developed a technique for dealing with her: he thought of her as being a sort of possession of Malcolm's, and the sensuality in her glance, her smile, was filtered through Malcolm's presence, scarcely reaching him.

He had little contact with the other females in the theater group, although in addition to the two in the cast there were enough of them around—minding the box office, sealing flyers to be sent out, telephoning, working on publicity, painting flats with Maryellen. Ferguson rather kept his distance from them all. It was with the male members of the group—as he would have expected—that he developed something of a feeling of camaraderie.

But his relationship with Gene Mack did not improve.

Mack's problem, Fergie soon discovered, was that he aspired to belong socially in Chillingworth. He didn't want to be only the town's servant, a cop in a car, but wished to be one of the intelligentsia, a peer in a top group. Why the man cared about such things Fergie couldn't imagine, but he seemed to believe that being accepted as a member of the theater company would automatically admit him to local top-drawer society. He accordingly saw the appointment of Ferguson Brady to the post of "artistic adviser" as a nudge downward for himself—a reduction in rank from scenery

36

coordinator to carpenter.

Ferguson hoped that in time they would get along—when they got to know one another better.

Whereas he had spent the last four years almost entirely alone, except for his dog and the cats, now suddenly Ferguson found his life crowded with people. Not only was there the theater group, there was also Alice.

Not that Alice made anything seem crowded, but he was not at ease with her anymore, as he had once been. He was only comfortable, really, with Malcolm or with Frank Wells.

After her first visit, it had been several days before Alice appeared again. He'd thought of bicycling over to see her, but some reluctance he couldn't put his finger on had prevented him from going. And then one morning she drove over and came looking for him in his workshop.

The old carriage-house door opened and she came through it. He stopped sanding the piece of maple under his hands. But she did not speak until she'd wandered all around, looking at everything he'd been working on.

"I heard you were doing this." She paused at the chair, the second of the side chairs for his dining room—he was still laboring over the finish. "This is beautiful!"

"It's part of a set of furniture I designed for myself."

"You designed it! I'd heard only that you were making reproductions of antiques—for some of your mother's old customers. Well, no wonder you quit the bank. If you can do something like this . . ."

"I'm glad you like it." He took her into the house so that she could see the table, and he was properly gratified at her reaction.

"I came over to ask you a favor," she said when, as before, she had made them some coffee in the kitchen.

He gazed with amazement again at the fascinating hollows in her cheeks and tried to keep his eyes away from the cleavage revealed below the unbuttoned third button of her shirt.

"Sure, Alice. Anything."

"Well, there I am with that whole big house and no furniture. The kitchen appliances are in it, luckily, and I bought box springs and a mattress at Bloomingdale's to go on a bed I found at the Goodwill. But aside from that I haven't even a rag rug."

"Take some of my stuff. You told me I've got too much in here. Pick anything that appeals to you."

"Oh, I couldn't do that! I didn't come to cadge, beg, or borrow. I thought you could advise me as to which of the second-hand or antique dealers might have a few things at a decent price."

"I can advise you—easy. But I meant the other, too. You're right that this house is like a stockroom. It's got every period of furniture stuck in next to each other, looking a mess."

"I'll make a deal with you. Let me help you get this place whipped into shape—redecorated and rearranged, and the overflow sold off. In return you give me a healthy discount on the pieces I'd like to have and that you don't want. Between us we should be able to figure out what they're worth."

"Fine. Only I wouldn't let you pay me, Alice. You'll have more than earned whatever you take."

"Well . . . we can talk about that later. Let's take a look, for a start, and find out whether you think some such project will work."

She stood in the living room for a few minutes, frowning, glancing around. "The cats can all adjust, I hope, if I suggest doing away with one or another of their favorite sleeping places." Her tone suggested that they would have no choice —though it wasn't, he thought, as if she didn't like Mitzi and the kittens.

"Oh, sure." Two of them were sleeping on chairs and Mitzi, he could see, was napping inside an eighteenth-century cabinet whose bottom door she knew how to open.

Alice asked for pen and paper and began four lists: what Fergie should keep, what definitely should go, undecided, and items she would like for herself.

She worked so fast she made his head swim.

"Who might give you the best price for these things you're getting rid of?"

"Depends on the item. I can take the list around and see what I'm offered."

"I'll go with you. I've a feeling you might let yourself be beaten down."

She was right, of course. Bargaining made him uncomfortable and he was apt to give way.

"Now, what about these things I've picked for me, Gus?" There were a maple love seat, a desk, a hope chest, a cobbler's bench, a small chest of drawers, a couple of little tables, an assortment of chairs, some stools. Some of the better pieces he felt she could use she refused to take because they were too valuable.

"You said they were all things you don't want to keep, but are you sure?"

"Positive. Everything you've listed there for yourself is suitable for your house but not for mine. There's such a difference in feeling, after all, between colonial and Victorian." The present Ferguson house had been built in the eighteen seventies, after the original farmhouse down by the barn had been razed by fire. It had a nice Gothic feeling on the outside, and a gloomy interior heavily decorated with carved woodwork—pillared doorways, archways festooned at the top with wooden lace, fireplaces like the facades of Grecian temples. Colored light fell through stained glass windows on either side of the front door, and in the stairwell, and in the music room. And try as he would, Fergie couldn't imagine the place without its clutter.

"I feel like a thief," Alice said, "but I'll get my pieces out of here as soon as I can."

"How are you going to move them?"

"I expect Chris Durham can help me out. He's got a station wagon."

Fergie frowned. "Chris Durham? I wasn't aware you knew him."

"He lives practically next door to me. And he's almost knocked me down, offering assistance."

"Oh. Yes, I see." He did indeed. And he was far from trusting Durham's motives. He thought of mentioning to her that her helpful neighbor was married, though giving the impression these days that he was on the loose.

Well, he didn't backbite, and Alice was a grownup now.

That evening Durham came over with Alice to pick up some of her furniture.

"Yes, Ferguson's being a terrific help to us at the theater," Chris said to Alice as they loaded things into the back of the station wagon—and more in a similar vein, talking fulsomely about him as if Fergie were deaf or absent.

As she prepared to depart, Alice laid her hand on Fergie's arm, making him disconcertingly aware of her physical presence. "I'll be over tomorrow, if that's convenient, to take you around to dealers—see what kind of prices you can get."

40

"Okay. Sure." For the first time in years he felt embarrassed that he didn't drive. It didn't seem right for Alice to have to chauffeur him around.

"Why don't you apply for a driver's license, Gus, and buy a car?"

"I just don't want to."

"But that accident was years ago! How long ago—twelve years?"

"Thirteen."

"Well, long enough. And it was established that you weren't at fault, the other driver was."

"I was the one who picked the route that night. Chad and Don wanted to take the shortcut over the hills, but I decided to stick with the main highway. If I hadn't . . ."

If he hadn't made that decision, Chad wouldn't have been dead at the age of nineteen, and Don left with a leg that ended a little above the knee. His two best friends . . . Don long gone from around here, too, leaving Fergie with an amputation of another kind, though the friendship had never again been the same after the accident. Fergie's sense of guilt had made Don's loss an intolerable burden to them both whenever they'd been together.

Drive a car again? Oh, no!

They were on their way to Carlotta Snead's antique shop on Route Seven. Carlotta had been both a competitor and a friend of his mother's and probably remembered in detail most of what Gladys had had in her house. They reached the place, a big yellow clapboard house with white shutters and a fanlight over the door. Alice pulled into the drive.

She turned off the engine, but she made no move to get out.

"You can't go on living your life this way. It's infantile."

41

She had fixed him with a gaze of missionary zeal.

"It's not infantile. I don't want to be responsible for something terrible happening to anyone else—again."

"So at an age when you should be an adult, you've curled up in the womb and refuse to come out."

"That's not true. I absolutely do not want to be responsible for—"

"One of the chief differences between maturity and immaturity is the ability to be responsible—to *handle* responsibility regardless of what goes wrong."

"Alice, you're picking on me."

"You're damn right I am. Don't you know that things go wrong for people regardless of what you personally are doing? You're being very childish—completely self-centered —if you think you can make everyone else safe by not making any decisions, not taking any responsibility yourself.

"What you're really doing is trying to avoid guilt. Because you've suffered too much from guilt already—isn't that right?"

"Alice, you're a witch. But you're not going to argue me into anything, because I'm not listening to you."

He got out of the car and went into Lotta's shop, which was almost indistinguishable from his own living room.

Alice followed him in.

He had a terrible sinking feeling as he looked at her across a thicket of chairbacks flanked by a dropleaf table whose top was completely obscured by a collection of salts, porcelain figurines, candelabra, cut glass dishes, cruets, snuff boxes, candle snuffers, silver compotes, demitasse cups, mustache cups, letter openers, stacks of plates, and God knew what else.

Alice was going to ruin his life.

FIVE

And then, about a week before *Golden Boy* was to open, Malcolm and Maryellen broke up.

This occurrence should not have affected Fergie, but it did: Maryellen kept trotting up to his workshop when Malcolm was there, with some nonexistent problem about the set. She hung around, casting covert glances at Malcolm, until finally one afternoon he flung off in a fury.

"It's bad enough I have to see her at the theater all the time. Does she have to follow me up here?" he said between clenched teeth to Fergie. "I'll be back when she learns to stay home—or out of my way someplace else!" Gravel spurted from under the tires of his car, and he all but knocked the bark off a tree on his way down to the road.

A couple of days passed and he did not come back. Ferguson saw him down at the barn, where rehearsals were going forward early and late in an atmosphere of increasing urgency (opening night was coming up fast now—Thursday of next week), but he had little to say and seemed preoccupied.

Ferguson meanwhile was saddled with Maryellen. She followed him around like a lost puppy.

"He doesn't even *say* why he won't go out with me anymore," she complained to him on Saturday.

The action was all at the barn, where a rehearsal was scheduled, but here she was with him in his workshop.

"Maybe he'll change his mind then."

"You're sure he hasn't discussed me with you? He thinks such a lot of you, you know."

"He certainly wouldn't confide in me about his love life. Run along, Maryellen—I'm sure Chris needs you at the barn."

"No, he doesn't."

Well, he had no answer to that. The *Golden Boy* set was all painted, only waiting for the rest of the furniture, which was to be picked up on Monday. The desk table had long since been hauled down in a station wagon from Fergie's house—he was happy to spare it, as it was on Alice's list of things to get rid of—and the company was managing temporarily with folding chairs. Maryellen's job for this play was completed.

"Frank Wells says I ought to just forget Malcolm." She frowned at him from her seat on a bench under the window as he rubbed more linseed oil into the dining-room side chair. "He said to me just today, 'He's not your type, Maryellen.' Why, do you think?"

Ferguson shrugged, bored to the point of nausea by the subject.

"Do you think Frank knows something I don't know? Like Malcolm's going out with someone else and I just haven't found out about it?"

"I doubt it. Frank's only giving you fatherly advice. No use wasting your life regretting one fella when there are lots more around."

But tears stood in her eyes. "People your age don't understand—Frank, you. You don't even remember what it's like."

Though he certainly didn't want Maryellen cozying up to him as a potentially desirable sex object, he was far from pleased to find himself bracketed with a man of forty some-odd, the father of three children.

To Maryellen he was an old man.

"You're how old?" he asked her.

"Seventeen."

He heard the workshop door open and turned to see Alice crossing toward him, with Monty. The dog was used to her now—he didn't bark when she arrived.

He became aware abruptly of a chill in the atmosphere. Monty noticed it, too; he looked questioningly at his master.

Like two cats meeting for the first time—Alice and Maryellen. He stammered an introduction.

Or had he been mistaken? he wondered a minute later. Alice seemed the soul of friendliness.

Astonishingly, Maryellen left almost immediately.

"How did you do that?"

"Do what?"

"Get rid of her. I've been trying to get her to go for an hour."

"Have you? I can see why your mother warned you about girls. She'd turn in her grave if she saw you talking to that one."

"You don't drive a car?" Gene Mack stared at him as if he'd just discovered that Ferguson's head came to a point.

"No."

Gene's eyebrows quirked into one of their squiggly posi-

45

tions. "How did you lose your license?"

"I voluntarily failed to renew it. About thirteen years ago."

It had been taken away from him at the time of the accident, of course, but the privilege of applying for a license again had been restored to him after the hearing—none of which he felt like explaining to Officer Gene Mack.

"Well, no problem." Gene smiled, almost pleasantly. "I'll borrow a pickup truck from a friend of mine, and you can ride along and show me which pieces you chose for us."

So on Monday Fergie rode along.

He had found just what they needed for the sets—some of it in his own living room, some on his expeditions with Alice, some when he'd pedalled around to a few places on his bicycle.

While they were collecting the sofa and a couple of dining-room chairs from Lotta Snead's shop (Lotta had a felicitous range of quality in her place: everything from practically priceless down to what looked like Goodwill discards, over all of which she ferociously watched like a fat old dragon), he pointed out some of the things he'd picked for the *Blythe Spirit* set.

And it was at that point that he discovered the divergence of his ideas and Mack's on how a charming living room in Kent should look.

"Why not this?" Gene patted the carved back of a particularly hideous sofa. "And this?" Admiring a great, heavy breakfront. "It seems to me they'd be terrific—much better than . . ."

It was not long before Ferguson realized exactly why Chris Durham had wanted someone besides Gene working on putting the sets together. What kept recurring to him as he and his cohort haggled over one piece after another was a favorite

46

pronouncement of his mother's. "His taste's all in his mouth," she used to say.

His cousin Leona and Gene Mack would have made a wonderful couple, decoratorwise.

And then all the putting together of *Golden Boy* was over.

Final dress rehearsal on Wednesday. A disaster. Malcolm forgot his lines, Frank walked through his part like a zombie, Marta Guild stomped off the stage in the middle of Act Two and said she wasn't going on again. Ralph Mason, who played Roxy, lost his temper and pulled the door at stage-left halfway off its hinges so that it wouldn't close.

Ferguson went home with a feeling of gray disappointment settling over him. After what had seemed such a promising beginning, the production had simply come apart. The people were amateurs, after all, and now their lack of experience and lack of talent showed painfully.

Then on opening night Thursday he could hardly believe the polish, the assurance of the cast—the complete triumph of make-believe. He watched with Alice from out front—she'd insisted he get them seats together.

"I thought Chris would want you backstage, holding his hand," he had said rather sourly. Chris was always confiding to Ferguson that he and Alice had done this together, or that, had gone here, had gone there, as though this news must be of special interest to him.

"No. He wants my opinion afterward."

She was wearing a dress tonight, a sand-colored thing with a sort of yellow pattern around the bottom. How could he have thought she looked more female in pants and a shirt than she would in a dress?

Riding around with Alice to antique stores or sitting talking to her in his kitchen was not the same at all as appearing

47

with her at the theater, he discovered. She had driven over, they had met in front of the barn, and here he was, escorting her—if only down the aisle. He was aware of interested glances thrown their way as the two of them squeezed past the knees of those already seated to take their places in the middle of the row.

It was years since he'd taken a girl anywhere.

He thought of Sharon—another Maryellen, a girl like flypaper. If his mother hadn't gotten him out of that trouble . . .

Then Prudence. (Had he been drawn to her because of her name? After Sharon . . .) Prudence smiling shyly at him over the stacks of ones and fives and tens and twenties at the bank. He'd left her behind when he'd quit his teller's job. Gladly.

There had been no one since Prudence.

He was seated between Alice and Leona Wells—he and Frank had gotten their tickets at the same time. His cousin Leona—plump, pleasant, chubby-cheeked, with lips that were perennially pursed as though for a kiss—sat next to him with the kids lined up on the other side.

"Hello, Ferguson. My, I see you've come with a date." And calling across him, "Hello, Alice, I'd heard you were back in town . . ." She yakked on and on, no way to turn her off.

Even as he studied the printed program he was aware of heads turned, necks craned—people staring curiously to make sure they'd really seen Ferguson Brady with a girl. And then the house lights dimmed, a hush fell, and the play began.

There was a disturbence next to him. He glanced to one side to discover that Leona had changed places with one of the children, Dodie, who couldn't see past the tall man in front of her.

48

He was caught up, after that, in the emotions and problems of the characters on the stage.

The first park bench scene between Marta Guild and Malcolm was almost embarrassingly effective. Had some actual chemical attraction taken place, he wondered, during rehearsals? Was it this that had ended things between Mal and Maryellen? Though he had never seen the two of them hanging around together backstage . . .

At intermission the audience went outside into the warm June night. He was amazed at how many familiar faces he glimpsed in the crowd. He hadn't seen most of them in years. A few people spoke to him, some nodded, none lingered to engage him in conversation. In Chillingworth everyone minded his own business unless there was some good reason not to, like a disaster of some sort—fire, accident, sudden death. People here left you alone if you wanted to be left alone.

The majority of people around him, however, were strangers. From Wilton, maybe, or Westport or Weston. But some of them seemed to know each other—Chillingworth residents, then, new people.

Gene Mack was missing the performance tonight, he remembered—Mack currently had the midnight to eight A.M. shift and was now getting his sleep.

Alice took Fergie's arm as they went back in, and a small flash of brightness crossed his consciousness. For just a moment he was aware of a happy feeling of being like everyone else, a man like other men, someone who fitted in with the rest of the world. But the exhilaration lasted only briefly, and he was aware once again of the great difficulty of maintaining any kind of relationship with the rest of humanity without their either getting too close or remaining too far away.

He and Alice took their seats, and five-year-old Dodie

Wells immediately made him uncomfortable by staring at him with apparent dislike. He smiled at her but didn't know what to say.

The second act began. A couple of people fluffed their lines, but if he hadn't been to rehearsals, Ferguson wouldn't have known.

Then the third act—a great success—and the play was over. The curtain calls went on and on as the opening-night audience called the actors back for deafening applause. Last of all Chris came out and took a bow and thanked everyone: those who had helped in the conversion of the barn; the backstage workers; the advertisers who had made possible the printing of the program; the antique dealers who had supplied the furnishings for the set; the members of the zoning board who had allowed a variance so that Chillingworth could have a theater; the Chillingworth Theatre Foundation, which had provided financial backing; and in particular that great lady of the American stage, Miss Nadia Royal—long a local resident—who had made possible the purchase of the barn that had become the home of the Chillingworth Little Theatre.

"And now we invite you, ladies and gentlemen, to join our cast and all the members of the company in an opening-night celebration. There will be wine and cheese for everyone—oh, and lemonade for the younger portion of the audience."

Dodie Wells fell off the bench on which she was standing to try to see, and much against every natural inclination—since he knew nothing about dealing with children—Ferguson became involved in picking her up, examining her bleeding knee, and restoring her to her mother, who was talking to a friend in the aisle. By the time this good deed was accomplished, leaving him with an unexplained glow of warmth somewhere in his chest, Alice had disappeared.

50

He made his way backstage, past the line of people inching their way toward the refreshments being served down front.

To his surprise, Malcolm was talking with Maryellen. He caught sight of them in a secluded corner—Malcolm, his makeup still on, not trying to beat a retreat but speaking quite earnestly to the girl he'd been avoiding for the past week. Ferguson turned away, almost colliding with Ed Skinner, who played the part of Moody, the fight manager.

"A good performance, Ed. Congratulations."

"Thanks."

"Eddy, you were marvelous!" Donna Church, Alice's friend, rushed past Ferguson to throw herself into the arms of her fiancé. "Paul Newman better watch out!"

Ferguson found himself pushed to the edge of the stage, where Frank was leaning over to talk to Leona below him.

"She looks ready for bed." Frank nodded at Dodie, still snuffling as she clung to her mother's hand. "And you, young lady"—he frowned ferociously at Jenny, his eldest, who already stood taller than her mother—"where did you get that glass of wine? You're under age!"

Jenny, her father's favorite, smirked up at him. "I must look eighteen, I guess."

"Where's Daddy?" Dodie quavered, staring up wide-eyed at Frank, who burst into a delighted laugh.

"This is my false face, Punkin—I put it on for the play. You didn't know me?"

But she was frightened by his makeup, which looked grotesque close up.

"You'd better take them home, Leona. Where's Jeffrey?"

Leona turned to scan the barn, over the heads of the winebibbers, for her middle child. There he was, Ferguson saw, running from aisle to aisle on a row of seats.

"Jeffrey! Stop that! Jeffrey, come here—we're going! See

you at home, Frank. Bye, Ferguson." Leona squeezed through the crowd, with the girls in tow, heading for the spot where Jeffrey had now disappeared.

"You were great, Frank," Ferguson said sincerely. "How you can be so convincing in the part of an Italian immigrant —in fact I'd never have thought you'd make an actor at all."

"It's easy. You ought to try acting, Ferguson."

"Not me! A little backstage stuff is plenty." He saw Alice on the far side of the set, standing with Chris.

"You never know till you try. Playing the part of some stage character can take you right out of yourself. It's like magic."

"You think I need to be taken out of myself?" he asked skeptically.

Frank put a hand on his shoulder. "Well, personally, I get sick and tired of just being me. I should spend my entire life filling prescriptions? We can't all quit our jobs the way you did."

"And we can't all step onto a stage and distinguish ourselves . . ."

By the time Fergie reached the place where Alice had been she was no longer there. Admirers clustered around Nadia Royal, but he did not join them. The closer he got the older she looked, and he felt he would rather preserve the memories of her garnered in earlier years from the other side of the footlights. He wandered about the stage, talked to the master electrician, the assistant property person, the stage manager, the production assistant; watched the bevy of apprentice actresses who did chores around the place, as they started collecting the disposable plastic glasses.

The last of the audience melted away, except for those who would be leaving with members of the cast—Lucy Cannon's husband, Marta Guild's boyfriend, Ed's fiancée Donna

Church—oh, there was Alice at last, talking to Donna—and to Chris.

"Shall we go out and celebrate?" he heard Chris asking Alice as he came up to them. "I've got to drop off the box office take at the night depository down in Wilton, but we could go on to—"

"Not me, thanks. If you want to celebrate, why not do it with the cast?"

Ferguson observed with pleasure the disappointment in Durham's arrogant face. Though he had managed to work with Chris, everything the man did still rubbed him the wrong way. And what he disliked most of all was his proprietary air with Alice.

It was Ferguson who walked her out to her car.

"Alice . . ."

She looked up expectantly. "Yes?"

"It's not my affair—I know that—but it bothers me to see you getting involved with Chris Durham, when he's married."

In the illumination from the floodlights mounted on the side of the barn her smile was faintly amused. "You didn't seem at all distressed to hear about my living with a man in New York, without benefit of a wedding ring. It would be another matter altogether if you thought I was sleeping with a man who was married to someone else?"

"I'm not making moral judgments!" He was surprised at his own anger. He waited a moment and said more calmly, "I'm concerned about you, that's all. Because we've always been friends."

"We've always been friends," she repeated after him, though with a touch of acid in her voice. "And one is always thankful for friends." For some reason she seemed exasperated with him.

She gave a ragged sigh. "I'm not sleeping with Chris Durham. And if it makes you feel any better about things, his wife's filing for divorce."

"Oh."

"On the grounds that the marriage has 'irretrievably broken down.' That's grounds, now, in Connecticut—no struggle, no name-calling, no placing the blame or anything." She extracted her key ring from her bag. "Can I give you a lift home?"

"Thanks—no, I'll walk. It's a nice night."

She got into her car. He closed the door and she leaned her arm on the open window, looking up at him. "Your attack folded up awfully easy there."

"I wasn't attacking you, Alice," he said gently.

"No, you were attacking Chris."

He thought for a minute. "You want me to tell him off for you? I *can.*" Gladly.

"No." She seemed a little hesitant. "That's not what I want . . ."

A pair of headlight beams arced over him as a car pulled out nearby and went slowly past. He saw that the driver was Durham. Ferguson watched as the theater director drove out to the highway and headed south.

Alice had turned on her engine. She put on the headlights. "Well, goodnight, Gus."

The name pleased him every time she used it, for some reason summoning up a self-image of someone taller and more forceful than any character named Ferguson could ever be.

"Night, Alice." He stepped back and Alice followed Chris out the drive, turning the opposite way, north, toward home.

Nearly everyone had gone. Only three cars were still parked in the lot—one of them Maryellen's, the second-hand

54

purple Volkswagen covered with pink daisy decals. It had been a graduation present this spring. The VW sat alone near the rear door that led backstage.

Ferguson glanced in as he walked past it toward the path across the field. She was sitting behind the wheel, by herself.

He stopped.

"Maryellen?"

She turned and looked at him without speaking.

"You waiting for someone?"

"No." She'd been crying and her voice was muffled. "There's no one to wait for."

Things hadn't been patched up, then, with Malcolm.

"Did your family see the play tonight?" he asked, to change the subject.

"No, they're coming Saturday." She looked distractedly about her in the car and then got out and started toward the back door into the barn.

"Hey! Where you going?" he called after her.

"I forgot. I left my sister's sweater backstage—she'll kill me."

He watched her fumbling in her drawstring purse for the key, as the door had already been locked. She found it, opened the door, and slipped in.

"Goodnight, Maryellen," he called to her as she stood in the darkness of backstage, silhouetted dimly for a moment against the lighted auditorium beyond.

The door clicked shut and Ferguson turned toward the fence at the back of the parking lot, skinned between the top and bottom rails, and started on his way across the field toward home.

SIX

Fergie had been watching an old Gable movie, *The Misfits*, on television when the first call came. It was Mrs. Polk, Maryellen's mother, phoning him.

"She hasn't come home." A tremor of nervousness in her voice. He had never met Mrs. Polk or Mr. Polk—the Polks were new people in town, had only lived there four or five years. "She told us she's been working with you at the theater, and I wondered whether you knew . . ."

"I'm sorry, Mrs. Polk, but I haven't seen her since right after the performance."

"Oh. I see."

"I spoke to Maryellen in the parking lot, and then she went back inside to get a sweater she'd left. That's the last I saw of her."

"Oh. Well, I'm sorry to have bothered you."

"Have you tried calling Malcolm Ludlow? She was talking with him earlier in the evening. He might have known what her plans were."

"He's not home. I've been dialing and dialing his number. If she's with him it's all right, but she should let me *know*

56

—it's nearly one-thirty . . ."

Yes. Twenty-five after one. No wonder she was worried, if she'd expected Maryellen home right after the final curtain.

A little later the phone rang again.

"Hi, this is Malcolm."

"Mal! Hey! Is Maryellen with you?"

"No. Of course not. I haven't seen her since I left the theater. Her mother just called me—I'd been out."

"Maryellen didn't tell you of any plans she had? I saw you talking—"

"Why would she tell me her plans? The whole conversation was her promising to get off my back. She said she knew we were really washed up, she just wanted to be friends. You didn't see her with anyone else, Ferguson? Somebody she might have taken off with?"

"You and me. She talked to both of us. I don't know who else. I only saw her for a couple of minutes."

"Yeh. Sure. Well, she'll turn up. Maybe she's found some new guy to latch onto." But he sounded uneasy.

There was a hollow feeling in Fergie's stomach when he hung up. He turned off the TV and went out to the kitchen for some kind of snack. But the hollow feeling wasn't just hunger.

He made some instant coffee, thinking of Alice and how she looked when she poured from the kettle into the mugs. He couldn't use the copper kettle anymore without Alice's coming to mind. He didn't know why he kept thinking so much about her. Probably because beautiful girls like that always upset him.

He cut a piece of Sara Lee chocolate cake, prized it out of its pleated aluminum setting, and bit into it.

Maryellen, too. Maryellen had always made him very nervous—being so terribly female. Females were like another genus, or at least a different species, from mankind. To him they were, anyhow. Was Alice right? Did he have some sort of hangup concerning his mother? That kind of thing might, he supposed, make it difficult for him to relate to other women as he should.

He took another square of cake, not remembering he'd eaten one—he had no recollection of it.

He thought of Sharon. She was from such a long time ago, when he had still been driving a car. It was impossible to deny that he had enjoyed all those things Sharon had encouraged him to do, but he had never connected with her as a personality. The whole affair had been pretty much on an animal level.

The first time he'd seen Maryellen, she had reminded him right away of Sharon. That same animalism . . .

He put the cover back on the cake, washed up his mug under the tap, dried it,and put it away. Might as well go up to bed.

He was down to his shorts when Monty, on the first floor where he always slept, started to bark. Ferguson put his pants and shirt back on and went out into the hall.

A car was coming up the drive; the stained glass of the upper hall window glowed with the colors of gems as it was struck by the headlight beams.

He thought of the pink daisies glowing against the dark of Maryellen's car in the illumination from the floodlights. He thought of Maryellen's small pointed breasts silhouetted against the lighted auditorium in the blackness of backstage just before the door had swung to.

He turned on the downstairs hall light from the switch at the top of the stairs and padded barefoot down the carpeted treads, with a feeling of tenseness in his stomach muscles, a certainty of evil to come in the marrow of his bones, and in the endings of the nerves in his hands and feet.

It was the police who had come.

It was nearly three in the morning when they found her. In Ferguson Brady's woods.

"Jesus!" Eugene Mack said to Buddy Swanzey, a part-time officer who had been called out to help search.

He stared down at the body sprawled in the bed of last year's oak leaves, at the distorted face, the swollen neck—something fastened around it . . . a belt? At the nude lower half of the torso, the still, contorted limbs.

"Raped for sure," said Buddy. He felt sick, looking at this thing lying there. Maryellen had been a friend of his sister's.

"I was so damn sure we'd find she was just out with some guy, making out in his car, and forgot to come home." Gene switched the flashlight back onto the path, away from what lay next to it. "You stay here. I'll go put in a call, get the Chief out here right away—and whoever else we need."

"And tell her family . . ."

"Yes—and inform her family. But the important thing is to get some equipment out here." Lights, a camera, an ambulance to take the body away. And the medical examiner—he'd need to see her first. "Don't touch anything, don't make any tracks you haven't already made . . ."

"Yeh."

"And you heard nothing? No screams?"

"No. I told you the television set was on. I was watching a movie . . . My dog barked, though—oh, for quite some time."

"When was that?"

59

"Let me see. It wasn't too long after I came home. He barked and barked, starting at—oh, maybe a little after twelve."

Ferguson sat in his living room with two officers, Chief of Police Hyslop and Eugene Mack.

"Did you let the dog out?" It was the chief of police—a red-faced blond man, well-built but rather compact, and pleasant-looking—who was asking the questions.

"No. I don't let him out at night because I don't want him bothering the deer."

The chief looked over at Monty, and Ferguson could see the thought registering in his mind that the animal was, yes, a deer hound.

"What time was it when you left the theater?"

"It must have been a little before twelve—maybe ten of? Because it was around midnight when I got home. I remember looking at the kitchen clock. The play ran long, it being the first night, then people hung around a while congratulating the cast. And everyone was served wine and cheese." Fergie was very much aware of Gene watching him as he talked.

"It was about ten of twelve, then, that you last saw Maryellen Polk as she unlocked the door and went back into the theater?"

"Very near that."

"How did she happen to have a key to the barn?"

"Chris Durham had given it to her. She needed it because she was working on the set for the play."

"So she went inside, closed the door after her—is that what you said?"

"Yes."

"And you walked home by way of the field and the woods."

60

"Yes."

"Which should have taken you how long?"

"Five minutes. I told you that."

"And it was midnight when you got home?"

"Yes."

"You say you left the theater at ten of twelve. If it took you five minutes to walk home, you've got five minutes unaccounted for there."

Ferguson tried to restrain his rising exasperation. "I said it was *about* ten of twelve when I last saw Maryellen. And *about* midnight when I got home. I didn't time myself with a stop watch. Maybe I was four minutes talking with Maryellen instead of two, and maybe it took me seven minutes to walk home instead of five, and maybe it was one minute of twelve when I looked at my kitchen clock."

"A lot of 'maybe's' aren't much help to us in a murder investigation, Mr. Brady."

"Look, you can check with Alice Jenner on the time I was last seen at the barn. I was talking to her just before my conversation with Maryellen. As Alice drive out I went over to Maryellen's car and spoke to her. Chris Durham might also remember the time—he drove past Alice and me as we were talking, and Alice's car followed his out of the parking lot."

"What about the other cars you say were still there. Do you know whose they were?"

"No. I only remember noticing that there were a couple of cars at the front of the lot. I didn't really look at them, I was just aware that someone must be still in the theater. And I do know someone remained inside, because the auditorium lights were on when Maryellen went in. I could see that much when she opened the door."

"After she'd gone in, did you wait for her to come out?"

"No—I told you. I started home by the path that leads across the field there and through my woods. Whoever was in the theater turned off the outside floodlights while I was crossing the field, and after that I heard voices behind me, both male and female. Then I heard either one or two cars start up and drive off. I looked back as I crossed the stone fence at the edge of the woods, and the place was dark. I assumed everyone had gone."

"You didn't go back to see whether Miss Polk might still be there?"

"No. Why should I? She had only gone in to get the sweater she'd left behind, which was no concern of mine."

"Yes, I see."

But did he?

SEVEN

Alice was curled up in a wing chair in her living room—one she had gotten from Ferguson and reupholstered. It was a sunny morning; the birds were noisy outside. Supposedly she was reading the "Help Wanted" ads in yesterday's *Norwalk Hour,* in hopes of finding some kind of interesting job, but actually she was meditating on whether she was any better off out here than in New York with Maury. At least her life there had had a pattern. Here she didn't know what to expect from the future, and the present seemed an unsatisfactory mess.

She wondered how much her long-ago fixation on Gus had influenced her decision to come back. The dreadful crush on him she had developed when she was working in the Antique Barn for his mother had survived everything, even analysis. How could she be so silly? He had never made a single move in her direction and never would. Girls turned him off—that was quite clear. Not, she thought, that fellas turned him on, but . . . Why was she so hung up on him? He still—even cowering in the far corner of the front seat of her car, as far from her as he could get—seemed to her like some marvelous combination of Robert Redford and the young William Holden.

There had to be a key to him—somewhere.

She heard a car going by. No—correction—she heard a car *not* going by. It had turned into the drive.

Chris? This early in the morning? She swivelled in her chair and, sure enough, she could see him through the window, getting out of his vintage station wagon.

She was puzzled, when she opened the door, to find him minus his usual cockiness, and she liked him better without it.

He seemed quite unstrung.

"What's wrong?"

"You didn't hear, then. Maryellen Polk was murdered last night."

"Oh, no!" A chill and a shudder went over her, followed by a wave of pity and a pang of guilt that she hadn't liked the girl.

"How?" she asked.

"Strangled. And I'd gather from the kind of questions the police have been asking me, raped as well. She never came home after the play last night, and they finally found her in the woods behind the theater."

"Woods?" She stepped back to let him into the hall and leaned against the wall. "There aren't any woods back of the barn. There's a field."

"On the other side of the field. Ferguson's woods. They found her near his house."

"Oh!" A nasty, jolting feeling. The picture of Maryellen with Gus, as she'd seen them the other day when she went into his workshop, floated suddenly before her. She put it out of her mind at once. "Have they any idea who? . . ." she asked. She had reached back and placed her hands against

64

the wall behind her, her palms against the sprigged, flowered paper as though she were leaning there for support. Her heartbeat had accelerated uncomfortably.

"If they have any leads, they didn't tell me. They've still got a lot of people to question. They'd already talked to Ferguson, of course—and to Malcolm, since he'd been going with her. But it could have been anyone—someone from out of town, even, who was in the audience and waited around after. Nobody'd even know his name, someone like that." He passed a hand across his brow. "Christ!"

"Did the police give you a hard time? You look as if you'd been through the war."

"Oh, they were okay—very polite, fine. In fact the officer in charge of the case, the one who actually found her, is one of our theater company. Gene Mack. He happened to be on duty last night—or this morning, rather, when the search was decided on.

"But the shock of this . . . That poor little kid. I've got to go over and talk to her parents. She was to have a part in the next production, you know. A nice one. She tried out for me and . . ." He turned away.

"I feel sick," he said hollowly.

"Can I come over?" Malcolm's voice, strained, over the phone. "Or are there police still there?"

"No," Ferguson told him, "they've gone. For now, anyway."

Malcolm came over.

He looked white and drawn—his eyes, as Ferguson's mother would have said, like holes burned in a blanket.

"No use my going to work today. I called in sick." Malcolm spoke as though words were an effort.

Ferguson put a hand on his shoulder. "I'm so sorry, Malcolm . . . about Maryellen. I know you must—"

"I feel rotten. She's been so unhappy this last week, and it was my fault. If I'd just have lied a little instead of telling her to get lost. If I'd known . . ."

If I'd known. How many times Ferguson had thought that same thing. If he'd known, he would have taken the other road; Chad and Don wouldn't have been . . .

"You mustn't reproach yourself, Mal. She'd have gotten over how she felt. The terrible thing is what happened to her."

"Yes. It's—it's unbelievable." They stood in the living room. Malcolm's eyes passed slowly over the hodgepodge collection of Gladys's furniture—the tables and stands less cumbered now with bric-a-brac—and down to the floor, almost as if he thought the terrible act had taken place there, in that room.

"Let's go outside," Ferguson suggested, himself oppressed by recollection of the police activity there during the early morning hours. Cigarette smoke still permeated the air.

They went out through the kitchen to the back porch, a long, narrow, railed area partially recessed under two of the upstairs bedrooms. There they sat on the Philadelphia bench, which had a view through the rose arbor to a listing sundial.

"I can't prove where I was, you know. I told the police I was at the Anchor Chain. I suppose they'll try to check that out."

"What's the Anchor Chain?"

"A bar down on the Post Road, edge of Norwalk. I've been there a couple of times. They've got a good band."

"Maybe someone'll remember they saw you there."

"Aaaaah!" Malcolm looked sideways at him and away again. "I should get so lucky." And something told Fergie

66

that the bar in Norwalk was not where Malcolm had been last night.

"The police can't think *you* did it. Anyone will tell them —in fact Gene Mack himself knows—"

"That I'd have gotten it for free, no need to rape her? Sure. But the fuzz know I'd quarreled with her, that she wouldn't get off my back. The way they see it, you quarrel bad enough somebody may get killed. Heat of the moment. I hope she doesn't come out pregnant when they do the autopsy, or they'll think she was after me to marry her and I didn't want to.

"She wasn't, as far as I know," he added defensively. "But then she might not have told me—yet."

"Quit worrying. Gene'll find it wasn't you. What's got you down is a feeling of guilt because you made Maryellen unhappy for a few days. Guilt can affect your whole outlook."

"Yeh, I suppose." Malcolm stared bleakly out through the rose arbor to the sundial. "All I can think of now, of course, is how much I really liked her. I wasn't mad at her actually, just annoyed because she wouldn't let me alone.

"I was attracted to her, sure. Who wouldn't be? But she wasn't my type. There wasn't anything you could talk to her about—she didn't know anything. She was just physical—all the time. Well, that's all right for a while; then you get the feeling you want to get away. It's—it was like drowning in a sea of marshmallow."

"I know what you mean. She wouldn't have been my type, either." My type if what, he asked himself mockingly. My type if she'd been old enough? My type if I went out with girls?

"What I keep thinking of is that she was killed that way."

"God, yes!" said Ferguson. "Such an ugly way to die."

"What I mean is the fact that she was murdered at all. Maryellen wasn't the kind of a girl who would get herself killed trying to protect her honor. I don't mean she was promiscuous, but I'd have guessed if anyone forced his attentions on her she would have been philosophical and let him go ahead—if she couldn't get away."

"So maybe she was killed because the guy gets his kicks that way?"

"Or else to stop her from telling afterward."

"Because he was someone she knew, you mean."

"Exactly."

Someone she knew, thought Fergie . . .

Ferguson had had to get out of the house after Malcolm left. The police might be back to ask him further questions or to tromp some more through his woods, and he'd had enough of the police for today.

He shut Monty in the house and took his bicycle down off the back porch. He'd go over to Alice's.

He went down the drive and then the short distance along Hill Road to the highway. It gave him a start to see that Maryellen's VW still sat in the parking lot by the barn, as though waiting for her to come back. The police would by now have examined it thoroughly, he supposed. For fingerprints, *et cetera*. For blood? He tried to remember whether he had touched the window edge when he'd stopped to talk to her. Chief Hyslop and Officer Mack knew he had talked with her then—they'd expect his prints to be there, wouldn't they?

He turned onto the highway, headed north. He felt very bad about Maryellen. The perfection of the June day seemed somehow cruel when you thought of her lying newly dead, her life cut short.

He passed the filling station, then the school on the left, and on the right the fire station and the town hall. At the corner he turned on Sachem Road. As he neared the railroad crossing, on an impulse he turned across the blacktop and glided into the parking lot that served the grocery and the drugstore on the near side of the tracks—Smithfield's Market, long established in a renovated warehouse, and the Chillingworth Pharmacy, in an old house. Both turned their backs to the rails and to the Victorian gingerbread station, which had been painted a dull barn red.

He left his bicycle in the rack and went into the drugstore, pleased, as always, at sight of the apothecary show globes suspended by their chains in either front window, the classical glass shapes filled with colored liquid, amber and turquoise. His mother had long ago found them for Frank, who had explained their purpose to Fergie: before there were electric signs, show globes had been used. With a candle lit behind them, they had shone out in glowing colors as a guide to those who—perhaps in desperate haste—sought the apothecary after dark.

There were no customers in the store. The one salesgirl was busy with something at the cosmetic counter, and both Frank and his young assistant pharmacist were working in the prescription department at the rear, behind the glass partition.

Ferguson went on back. Seeing him, Frank came out from amongst the ranks of pill bottles. No thespian, this morning —just a tired-looking druggist, his rather lumpy face even paler than usual beneath his dark hair.

"Well, Ferguson." He shook his head sadly. "What a terrible thing, eh?"

"Yeh. It's hard to believe."

"Little more than a child! You read in the papers about

those things happening, but when it's someone you know . . . and here in Chillingworth. We've never had a crime like that here. I've lived here half my life. Never anything like this . . ."

"You don't know, do you, Frank, who she might have been with?"

"No idea."

"I thought you might have seen her talking with someone."

"Only Malcolm, right after the performance. And obviously it couldn't have been him."

"No. He was just over at my place. He doesn't know anything either about what happened."

"Funny. I—" Frank's attention had shifted to his salesgirl, who was busying herself with the rearrangement of some jars on a nearby shelf and listening, no doubt, to every word they said. "Debra, you can neat up those greeting cards if you will, please."

Regretfully, Debra, a scrawny young woman with short straw-colored hair, retreated to the front of the store.

"It's funny, I was going to say. I don't understand how she got back in your woods. She must have gone willingly—in the first place, anyhow. With all the people there were in the parking lot getting into their cars after the performance, no one could have seized her and forcibly taken her across the field. They'd have been seen, or she would have screamed."

"That wasn't when it happened. It happened after everyone else had left the theater."

A frown on the pharmacist's wan face. "But Maryellen had gone by then." For the first time Ferguson took note of the long red scratch on Frank's cheek. He'd been subconsciously aware of it, he realized, but too preoccupied with thoughts of Maryellen's death to pay it any attention.

70

"I was the last one out of the theater," Frank went on, "and I *know* she wasn't there. Her car was still in the parking lot, but she wasn't in it. What makes you think . . ."

Ferguson told him of his parting conversation with Maryellen, and of her going back inside the barn.

"Why wouldn't I have seen her, then?" Frank looked worriedly at the plastic-coated table of Connecticut sales tax amounts which lay on the counter in front of him; he moved it to one side, neatly against the base of the cash register. "Chris had asked me to close up, because he wanted to get the box-office money down to the bank. I locked all the doors, checked backstage. No one was there but the Cannons —Lucy had taken a long time changing because a zipper stuck. She and Bill and I went out together."

"And you turned off the lights."

"That's right."

"The lights backstage were off when Maryellen went in, but the auditorium was still lit. I could see only her silhouette."

Frank sighed. "That's it, then. We must have been in the lobby—I'd have been standing at the panel of light switches, and the Cannons with me, waiting at the door, when Maryellen came in at the back." A little spasm of pity crossed his face. "I must have left the poor child in the dark to look for her sweater."

His finger—involuntarily, it seemed—touched the scratch on his cheek, traced it its full length.

"That's the timing, I'm sure," Ferguson agreed. "The outside floodlights went off while I was crossing the field behind the barn on my way home." Leaving Ferguson Brady, Frank would be thinking, the last person who was known to have seen Maryellen Polk alive. "I heard voices right after that— you and the Cannons, obviously."

71

"Yes. Lucy and Bill and I talked for a couple of minutes before getting into our cars—the lines we'd flubbed, that sort of thing." He shook his head, narrowed his eyes. "There wasn't another soul around. No one. Bill and I drove out, one right behind the other, and the only car still in the parking lot was Maryellen's. My headlights picked up the pink daisies as I pulled out."

"You didn't wonder why it was still there?"

Frank gave a grim little smile. "I'd seen her talking with Malcolm, as if they'd made up. I supposed she'd gone with him, and her car was just sitting there."

"Well, she definitely didn't go anywhere with Malcolm."

"So you said."

"And I'd asked her whether she was waiting for anyone. She told me she wasn't." *There's no one to wait for* . . .

Frank's eyes met his. "So who?"

A tremor passed over Ferguson. "I'm their best prospect, I imagine. Last one to see her, according to my own statement. And her body was found in my woods. Chief of Police Hyslop thinks it's strange I didn't hear the screams—summer night, the windows open . . ."

Frank reached across the counter to touch his arm briefly, reassuringly. "Don't worry, Ferguson. Before you came in here I thought I was the prime suspect." Again his finger found the red streak on his face. "This scratch . . ." He smiled a little sickly.

"Where'd you get it?"

"The answer's about as convincing as that old one about bumping into a door. I ran into a tree branch in the dark, while I was trying to round up Cal Berry's horses. They were loose in my yard again when I got home last night."

Ferguson laughed for the first time that day.

72

"There's a low place in the stone fence where they come through."

"You think the police didn't believe you? About the branch?"

"They're trained not to believe anybody. And Gene Mack, for one, wouldn't give his best friend the benefit of the doubt."

And certainly not his worst enemy.

"Gene's going to check my lawn for hoofprints. Maybe then he'll be convinced.

"Someday one of those horses is going to wander out onto the road at night and cause a bad accident."

Yes. Ferguson could visualize it—the dark shape looming suddenly in the headlight beams; the slamming on of brakes; the frantic animal leaping between the headlights, onto the hood (he had heard of that happening, the animal trying to jump over the obstacle); the sickening impact; the shattering of glass.

A customer had come in—a youngish woman in jeans, no one he recognized. She was approaching the back counter.

"Good morning, Frank. What a terrible thing . . ."

"See you, Frank," Ferguson said. He headed out the door.

He labored up Ross Ridge Road and pedalled into the drive of the weathered clapboard house with its bright turquoise shutters. Alice was on her knees under one of the front windows, weeding.

"Hi." She got up, tossing a handful of uprooted grass onto a pile of wilting greenery in a basket.

"I guess you've heard."

"Chris told me." Ah, yes—Chris. Her eyes searched his

73

face. (For signs of wear and tear? Of guilt?) "It's horrible, isn't it."

"Yeh."

"You must have had a harrowing night. I suppose they were combing the woods and everywhere . . ."

"Yes. Then they used my house for headquarters after they found her—detectives, deputies, the medical examiner." He dropped down to sit on the slab of stone that topped the front stoop two steps above the ground. "Before all that her mother had called me, trying to locate her. Then Malcolm called. He was over this morning. He's terribly upset, naturally."

"You and he have become pretty close friends, haven't you."

"I guess you could say that. He's been so interested in learning woodworking. I've showed him how to do a few things."

"I don't remember Malcolm from before we moved away —or his family."

"His family doesn't live here. He's from down in Westchester somewhere. He moved here when he got a job in the area. Lives in that studio Mrs. Seide rents out." Everyone around here was familiar with the studio the late Bernard Seide, the prominent sculptor—dead these twenty years— had built on his property across the drive from his house, which now, in this residential town zoned for one-family dwellings on two-acre plots, was the only "apartment" to be found in Chillingworth.

"Well," Alice said somberly, "I suppose it couldn't have been Malcolm who did her in. That wouldn't make sense."

He told her what he'd learned from Frank. "All of which boils down," he finished, "to the fact that I've got to be the number one suspect. The last three people, supposedly, who

74

were in the barn left together, and I'm the only one who even knew Maryellen was still there."

She looked at him, startled. "Good heavens, Gus! Don't go around saying things like that. You might give people the idea you could be guilty!

"I'd much rather suspect Frank Wells, myself—with a scratch on his face? He could have gone into Berry's pasture after he got home and shooed a couple of horses over the wall so that there *would* be hoofprints for the police to find."

"You don't seriously think Frank could have killed Maryellen?"

"How do I know? He's one of those quiet types that can be anything underneath."

And the same description fits me, Ferguson thought.

"The fact is, anyone could have come by on the highway." Alice frowned into the distance, a view of the hillside opposite, framed by a gap in the trees. "Or on your road. After you'd left the barn, after Frank Wells and the Cannons had left, anyone driving past could have seen Maryellen getting into her car all alone. Could have come into the parking lot and blocked her exit. Maybe that's why she ran into the woods—it was the only way she could go.

"What the police will do, I'm sure, is check on all the known—or suspected—local sex offenders."

"Um. Sure. What did Chris have to say? He called you this morning?"

"No, he came over. He was pretty shook. The police had been at his house asking him questions."

"Good."

She glanced at him sideways. "You don't like Chris?"

"Not much. He rubs me the wrong way."

"You mean that besides his potentially leading me astray, you don't like him anyhow."

"That's right."

"Heck. I thought maybe you'd taken against him because you had designs on me yourself. What a disappointment." Well, that was the way Alice talked sometimes. She wasn't trying to trap him into anything—she'd know better.

"Did Chris have any theory about the murder?"

"Well, as he said, it could have been done by anyone, even some guy from out of town that was in the audience and waited around afterward to see what he could pick up."

"If there was anyone hanging around after, he sure as hell hid his car—because it wasn't there."

EIGHT

Alice was right. A list of individuals who had previously been charged with sexual assault—including some who had served time for their offence—was being checked out. Included also were a few who were simply under suspicion for following young girls and trying unsuccessfully to pick them up, but against whom nothing had been proven.

And Officer Mack was at that moment sitting in Leona Wells's living room asking her about the horses. Since he had been on duty when the police search for Maryellen had been requested, and since he had been the one to find her, this was officially his case. And also, since this was the first crime of such seriousness to have been committed in Chillingworth in living memory (so he had already learned), he saw the investigation of which he was in charge as a unique and golden opportunity.

There was talk of promoting one of the six officers now under Chief of Police Hyslop to the rank of sergeant. He wanted to be that officer.

"No, I didn't see the horses," the druggist's wife said. "If they were in the yard when the children and I got home from the play, they must have been behind the house. The garage opens toward the front, as you must have noticed." She gestured in that direction with a plump hand whose nails were still crimsoned with the polish she had applied for her husband's opening night. "I just drove in, closed my garage door, opened Frank's for him, and got the kids right to bed —after bandaging my little girl's knee. She'd scraped it at the theater."

"You mightn't have seen the horses, but wouldn't you have heard them?"

"Not unless one of them got upset at something and neighed. They're very quiet. They just graze, you know. Pull up our good turf by the roots. That's what they come over here for, better grass."

"Do you remember what time it was when you got home?"

"It must have been eleven-thirty. I remember thinking how late it was for Dodie to be up."

"And what time was it when your husband got home?"

Leona Wells shook her head of black, curly hair. "I didn't hear him come in. He would have stayed quite a while at the theater, because everyone was congratulating the cast on their performances, and all of them were rehashing the play. I left early because of the children. After all, it was a school night."

"Yes, I see."

"Mr. Sayles, next door, may know what time Frank got back. He was out helping him with the horses. Burton wouldn't be home now, of course—he'd be at the funeral parlor."

Oh—*that* Sayles. The man who ran the mortuary. Many a time it was Gene's duty to drive up to the imposing white-columned building just north of Chillingworth and stop traffic on the highway while the funeral cortege came out the

78

gates and got under way.

So Gene Mack inspected the hoofprints to be found in the back yard, together with some of the damaged turf Mrs. Wells had mentioned. He also checked the low place in the stone fence, which had been blocked up with a couple of rocks and a dead branch. There were any number of low-hanging tree limbs, he noted, not to mention a couple of recently pruned forsythia bushes that could easily cause a facial scratch to anyone clumping about in the dark.

He managed to parry Mrs. Wells's avidly interested questions about the murder, at the same time assuring her that his call on her was strictly routine. Indeed, he wished that it were not, that it was something more, such as the pursuit of a really hot lead.

He thanked her, left her standing by the children's swing set in the back yard, and went around the corner of the house to where his official car sat in the drive. He walked past it and across the grass toward the Sayles house, noting another semicircular imprint of a horseshoe in a patch of damp ground, and farther on a deposit of fresh manure.

A long row of evergreen trees marked the front half of the property line, ending just short of the Sayles garage. He cut through between the evergreens and a clump of white birch, crossed the drive, and rang the bell of the rather pretentious pink brick mansion.

But no one was at home.

"I told you he wasn't there," Frank Wells's wife volunteered as he got into his car. She stood in the door of the enclosed breezeway of her neat cedar-shingle house.

"Well, I thought his wife or someone . . ."

Leona Wells's plump cheeks curved as she smiled. "He doesn't have a wife. They were divorced." He didn't know whether she was pleased because of the divorce or because she'd been able to supply him with further information.

"I see. Thank you."

In the distance a horse whinnied.

The carpeting on the floors of the Sayles Funeral Home was as thick and soft as, presumably, one's footing in the clouds in the hereafter. And no matter how shabbily one might have lived, the plushness of the mortuary furnishings assured one—if finally processed here—of an opulent departure from terrestrial existence.

Raymond Sayles was long dead, and his son, Vincent, was retired. It was Vincent's son Burton who ran the establishment now, with a cousin on his mother's side and a young man named Johnson, who was a recent graduate of mortician school.

There was to be a service in the chapel in half an hour, but Burton Sayles was able to speak for a few minutes with Officer Mack.

"How can I help you?" He looked born to the business, a bloodless, dignified man, probably about forty. He had nodded to Gene at a distance on occasion, while supervising the loading of a casket into the hearse, but they had never actually met. It was the young guy, Johnson, and the hearse drivers with whom Gene was acquainted.

"It's about the death last night—or this morning—of Maryellen Polk."

"Oh, yes. A tragedy." But of course Burton Sayles dealt all the time with sudden death and those affected by it.

"Did you know the girl?"

"To my knowledge we had never met. However, I am handling the arrangements here for the family. I don't believe I've met Mr. and Mrs. Polk, either. They're coming in this afternoon."

"Were you at the theater last night for the performance?"

"No. I have a ticket for this evening—though whether they will—"

"What I really wanted to ask you about, Mr. Sayles, concerns your next-door neighbor, Frank Wells. He referred me to you."

"Yes?" The tall, neat, dark-haired funeral director leaned forward in his chair as though in sympathy. Habit, no doubt.

"You saw Mr. Wells late last evening?"

"Yes. He came to the door to tell me some of the horses from the riding stable were loose on our side of the stone fence. I went out with him and we chased around after them and got them back into Berry's pasture. We each caught one, and the third followed the others over the wall. Someone had knocked a couple of stones off the top of the wall, making it just low enough. Kids—or the horses, possibly. We got the stones back on top and braced a fallen tree branch across the low spot."

"The horses have come through there before?"

"They do every once in a while."

"Only three horses, you said?"

"That's all we saw." Burton Sayles smiled, showing a beautiful set of white teeth—real, with a glint of silver from a molar. "But you try catching three horses that don't know you, and you'll find it's quite a job."

"What time was this that Mr. Wells came to your door?"

Mr. Sayles glanced at his watch. Thinking of the service to come, no doubt. "What time. Let me think." He looked back at Gene. "I was watching television . . ."

"Do you remember what program?"

"A documentary on Channel Thirteen. It started at eleven, and I missed the end because of the horses. I guess it must have been near twelve, because it was almost over. Five of twelve?"

"That sounds close enough. One more thing. Did Mr. Wells have a mark on his face when he came to your door? Bruise, scratch, anything?"

Sayles frowned and again consulted his watch. "Not that I remember. I'm sorry, but I must go, Officer Mack. I'll be needed for the service. Mr. Alvin Crumb . . ."

"Oh, yes." A long-time resident of Chillingworth of about eighty-five who had died of a heart attack.

The two of them came out of the elegant, panelled office where they had talked, and Sayles steered his visitor to a side entrance instead of the front door by which mourners were already arriving for Mr. Crumb's funeral.

"How long did it take the two of you, Mr. Sayles, to cope with the livestock?"

Burton Sayles thought back. "Oh, I suppose the better part of an hour."

"Why didn't you call up somebody at the Berrys' to come and take care of them? It's their responsibility."

For the first time, the tall, proper man he was questioning looked disconcerted. "Well, I don't know. I have called them in the past—told them to come and get their animals. For some reason Frank didn't want to call Cal Berry. He didn't say why."

"I see. Well, thanks."

Gene Mack went out past the empty hearse—which stood backed up ready for the coffin after the service—got into his car and headed to the Chillingworth Pharmacy to ask Frank Wells another question.

"Why didn't you telephone Mr. Berry—have him come over and get those horses out of there? It's simple, you know.

82

He'd just bring a bucket of oats and bang on it with a ladle, and the horses would follow him over the wall like he was the Pied Piper."

Frank Wells nodded. "I know. He'd just send his eldest girl, Frannie, over with the bucket. But I've had trouble with Cal Berry, one time and another. I'd rather not call him."

"What kind of trouble?"

"He's accused my kids of being the ones that let the horses out."

"A performance tonight? You can't mean it, Chris!"

The ring of the phone had gotten Malcolm out of bed. Not that he'd been asleep. He'd been hovering in a sort of limbo, trying not to think of either the past or the future—trying, in fact, to visualize some other life for himself than this one, a life far away, doing something quite different . . .

"Of course I mean it."

(What time was it, anyway? Nearly two in the afternoon . . . Malcolm took a deep breath. He was calming down a little, his pulse slowing now after the gallop it had gone into when the phone rang. He'd thought it would be the police again. Or his mother calling from White Plains. How long would it be before she heard what had happened? Would she call? . . .)

"I know this has been rough on you, Malcolm. After all, when you'd been going with the girl up till a few days ago . . . But if we don't give a performance tonight, the Chillingworth Little Theatre might as well close up shop—we'll have had it. It's hard enough to launch a project like this in the first place. If people that have supported us by buying tickets show up for our second performance—some of them coming from quite a distance—and find that—"

"Yeh, sure. But doesn't it seem pretty callous? . . ."

"I'm going to give a little curtain speech—not mentioning her by name, but referring to the tragedy."

For the capacity audience, Malcolm filled in for himself. Would Chris advertise it over the radio, too, he wondered—*Performance tonight at scene of rape slaying?*

"Well, you'll have to count me out. By tomorrow I could go on, probably. But today, no. Wayne should be delighted at the chance."

"I hope he can do it."

"That's what understudies are for."

"I'll call you tomorrow, then—see how you feel about Saturday's performances—and Sunday's." *Golden Boy* was to run for three weeks, Thursday through Sunday, with two shows daily on the weekends.

"Sure. Call me tomorrow."

He hung up and slumped into one of Mrs. Seide's rump-sprung easy chairs, from which he stared dully out the window.

Would-be standees were turned away. There was no place for them to stand without interfering with the sit-down audience.

They stood instead in the lobby, and milled around in the parking lot, watching everything with beady-eyed interest. After the play started, they were run off by a deputy policeman, and as they departed their license numbers were recorded, to be checked by computer against the file of marker numbers belonging to suspected sex offenders.

Of the cast, only Malcolm Ludlow was unable to go on. His role was played by the young man who was his understudy.

Burton Sayles attended the performance, although as things had turned out, he would rather not have gone.

He had no choice. He'd told the cop he had a ticket for tonight, and it would look strange if he did not attend—in case, that is, they were checking on him.

Burton Sayles was a very careful man.

And so he sat in the fourth row center and hardly saw what happened on the stage, because his mind was elsewhere.

When Alice went to bed that night she was aware, for the first time in years, of just how creaky the old Jenner house was.

As a very small girl she had lain terrified on many nights, listening in the dark to creaks on the stairs and in the hall that came closer, closer to her door; afraid to close her eyes for fear something might grab her before she knew it was there, afraid to keep them open for fear of what she might see.

It had not been real, flesh-and-blood things she had feared, but a fiery-eyed skeleton that could walk, that could come through closed doors. And she had lain straight and stiff in the middle of her bed to keep as far as possible from the demon arms of the things on the floor under the springs that could reach up and clutch at her.

But tonight it was no fiery-eyed skeleton, no demon, no ghost that occupied her thoughts as the boards of the old house creaked—on the stair, in the hall, downstairs in the empty living room.

She turned on her light again and read until her eyes would no longer stay open. She resolutely thought of nothing as she tried to sleep, but when she fell asleep and dreamed, it was of Maryellen—except that *she* was Maryellen, and someone was choking her to death.

NINE

"You've never married, Mr. Brady."

He wasn't sure whether that was a comment or a question. They knew his marital status, past and present.

"No."

It was Saturday, a beautiful morning again, and he sat in the white-walled office of Chief of Police Hyslop in the ground-floor headquarters that had been set up for the police at the back of the town hall, where the building, which was built into a slope, became two stories instead of one as it was in front. Chief Hyslop sat behind his desk, and Fergie in a straight-back chair beside it. Officer Gene Mack leaned against the wall behind Fergie.

Hyslop was asking the questions.

"Thirty-two. Most men are married by the time they reach your age."

He was tempted to say he didn't care much for girls, but Chief Hyslop might draw some quite unpleasant conclusion from such a statement.

"A lot of people don't marry till late," he said instead. "Or not at all."

Hyslop was leafing through some typed pages that lay before him. "I find you have from time to time taken an interest in girls." He raised his glance and his rather hard blue eyes rested on Ferguson. "Quite young girls. Like Maryellen Polk, for instance. I understand you and she have been spending a great deal of time together."

"Not a 'great deal,' Chief Hyslop, *some* time. We've been working on the set for the play—the *Golden Boy* set."

"That was constructed at the theater, not in your workshop. Yet Maryellen Polk was constantly at your house. This information comes from several different sources."

Including certainly and primarily Gene Mack. "Well, yes, she has been at my house—or rather, at my workshop. Sometimes conferring about the set, deciding things."

"All business, you mean. Nothing personal between you on her visits to your house—or your workshop?"

"Nothing personal between Maryellen and me. No."

"Yet other members of the theater group have indicated that a close personal relationship had developed between you and Miss Polk. Isn't that true now, Mr. Brady? Weren't you her new boyfriend? Or trying to be?"

"No!" He turned to Gene Mack, with whom this guess must have originated. Arms crossed, the master carpenter of the Chillingworth Little Theatre stared upwards at the ceiling, as if he had no part in this affair.

So Fergie made his explanation to Hyslop. "The only thing personal between Maryellen and me concerned Malcolm Ludlow. She and Malcolm had been going together until a few days ago, and then they broke up, as you must already have learned. Maryellen kept talking to me about it because Malcolm and I were friends. She thought I could help her figure out what had gone wrong—or even help to patch things up. She believed I had influence with Malcolm, I guess, and could change his mind for him."

"Did you suggest to her that you could help her in some such way?"

"Certainly not. I tried to discourage her—"

"Did you, Mr. Brady? I find that hard to believe—that you tried in any way to discourage Miss Polk. I suggest instead that you did everything in your power to ingratiate yourself with her, in the hope of succeeding Mr. Ludlow as her boyfriend."

"No!"

"And that when you failed to get what you wanted from her, you raped her and strangled her afterward. Isn't that what happened?"

Ferguson's skin was crawling. His stomach felt as though it had turned to quicksilver. "No. That's not what happened! I had *no* interest of that sort in Maryellen—"

"That's hard to believe, Mr. Brady. For a man with your . . . preference . . . for very young girls."

His hands were shaking now. He held them fast together, trying to keep them steady. "My preference? What preference? I haven't dated a girl in years!"

Chief of Police Hyslop's pleasant face showed a smile. "You're sure that's what you want to say? That you haven't dated a girl in years?"

"That's right."

"I thought you escorted Miss Alice Jenner to the play on—"

"Escorted? No. I bought her ticket for her, and we sat together. But she came alone to the theater and left the same way."

"So you're sticking with the statement that you 'haven't dated a girl in years.' "

"Yes."

"Exactly. That's one reason you're here now, being questioned, Mr. Brady." The slightly rasping voice had become a little harder. Ferguson braced himself for what was coming next. "If you were a usual, normal sort of man, you'd be married by now, or else dating some suitable girl—or girls. But—nothing?"

Ferguson felt his face burning.

The policeman's eyes narrowed. "What I'm getting at is this, Mr. Brady: you are now thirty-two years old, and have you ever in your life been interested in any girl over the age of seventeen?"

The anger welled up within him and overflowed. He got up from his chair, stood beside it with his hand gripping the back, and looked down at the man behind the desk. "You're trying to say that I'm a creep. A creep who's hung up on young girls. Sick in the head!" The blood was pounding furiously in his temples. "It isn't true! You're wrong! You'll find no proof of anything like that! Not a thing!"

Chief of Police Hyslop frowned at him. "Sit down, Mr. Brady. If there's proof, we'll find it. If there isn't, we won't. That's one reason you're here, so that you can give us some more answers to our questions, so that we can clear this thing up—one way or the other."

One way or the other . . .

Ferguson sat down again in the chair.

Nothing had been cleared up. All Fergie could feel, as he pedalled home at noon, was that they were persecuting him.

They hadn't a shred of evidence to connect him with Maryellen's death, but they were taking his life style and whole past history and making it into the description of an eccentric with a taste for young female flesh.

He was the last person known to have seen her alive. There was that.

And she'd been found in his woods. There was that. Proximity. Opportunity.

As he passed the barn his eye was caught by the sign out front, swinging by two little chains from under the signboard for the theater. *Matinee Today.*

Would Malcolm be able to go on, he wondered?

He turned into Hill Road, cycled along it and then up his drive.

Maybe he should go down for the performance. He would feel better, he thought, to be with others to whom suspicion might conceivably attach in the matter of Maryellen's death.

Tragedy, too, was a kind of dreadful magnet. When so many of those who had known her were all going to be together at the barn, it was hardly possible to stay away.

Malcolm was there. Though he didn't look fit to appear in his part. Fergie found him in the dressing room applying his makeup.

"You all right, Mal?"

"Don't I look all right?" But he seemed detached, as though his attention were on something other than the mask-like face before him in the mirror or the questions of his friend.

"No. Not too good. You don't have to go on—"

"I *want* to go on."

"That's the spirit, Joe," Chris said from the doorway. Whenever they were in the theater, he addressed the members of his cast by their names in the play—part of getting them to identify with their roles.

The house was filled to capacity again. "Because we're that

good?" Ed Skinner asked Fergie as they stood together counting the seconds till curtain time, ". . . or because we've got a bunch of sensation seekers out there?"

"Well, it's a good production. Whether Clifford Odets really has enough appeal for today's well-heeled commuter crowd who've been weaned on *Hair* and *Oh! Calcutta!* to pack them in I'm not sure . . . "

Ed was one member of the cast who at least looked like a matinee idol, tall, with blond good looks, even though his makeup for this play had been applied with the intention of making him appear older and a trifle seedy.

Ed Skinner was out of the running as a candidate for Maryellen's killer, Fergie assumed. According to Alice, Donna Church's family had entertained her fiancé and a couple of other company members at a champagne supper at their house after the opening-night performance.

Who else, he wondered, was in the clear? The cast must number nearly twenty, of whom only two were women. Then there were all the fellas in the production end . . .

His eye lingered on Norman Bernstein, who played Siggie, waiting in the wings, and Peter Tarinelli, who had the role of Frank Bonaparte. Anson Berry, Sid Rumfeldt, Kevin Klaus . . .

None of them looked worried.

The play began.

Fergie, watching from backstage, wondered at first whether Malcolm was going to make it. Chris, too, seemed doubtful, listening with his head cocked, a frown on his usually confident face, to how Malcolm recited his way through the first scene's dialogue. His delivery was wooden; he spoke as though he barely remembered his lines.

But in the second scene, where Joe, after his first fight, comes out of the shadowed doorway to face his father, he was

91

suddenly electrifyingly good.

Ferguson watched in fascination. Malcolm was more intense; he seemed to be putting more into his role than he had before.

The stage went dark at the end of Act One, and as the house lights came up, Frank's exit from the set brought him right past Fergie. He stopped.

"Malcolm's certainly keyed awfully high." Frank's face wore a worried frown.

"Isn't that normal during a performance?"

"Not like this. I hope he doesn't crack."

Ferguson went in search of Malcolm, but he had disappeared. By the time he caught sight of Mal again the bell was sounding for the end of the intermission; he had time only to smile at him as he was being read some sort of lecture by Chris.

The second act was better than the first. Malcolm played with a kind of contained fury, his performance striking new sparks from the others on stage with him.

The third act was marvelous.

"What a terrific actor!" The words were wrenched out of Fergie before he knew he was saying them, as Malcolm finished the last scene of the play in which he would appear and exited with Marta Guild to the other side.

"That's not acting, that's Malcolm," Chris murmured soberly with a note of puzzlement. He gazed with eyes narrowed at his star as he stood behind the flat across from the one that sheltered them.

Tragedy must have tapped some wellspring in Malcolm that enabled him to act with greater insight into the character he was interpereting, Fergie thought. But whether the result was art or nature hardly mattered.

At the end of the performance the cast took bows again

and again—in pairs, in groups, singly. But it was Malcolm the audience wanted.

Chris signaled at last for the house lights to go up. Malcolm had just come back from taking his final call. There was no elation on his face—only the same mask he'd worn before the play had begun.

"You surely do not believe you can do that again for tonight's audience!" Chris said.

"Do what?" Malcolm asked.

"Put your guts into it as you just have. I suspect after that you've nothing left. An actor has to hold back—not spend it all in one bright flash."

Fergie listened. Was this any way to shape talent? Malcolm had excelled anything he had previously done, and he was being whipped for it!

"But I was good, Chris! You know damn well I was!"

"Okay, you were good. You were great, but—"

"That's right. Today I'm Hamlet—couldn't you tell?"

Something about the words, Malcolm's narrowed eyes, a kind of fey air about him, gave Fergie an odd turn.

" 'The play's the thing'?" Chris said. "Well, you know what happened to Hamlet. Five acts, and he's carried out dead in the last one." He reached for Malcolm's wrist, held it up, peered at his fingers. Fergie could see that they were trembling.

"You're shot, Malcolm. For today, anyhow. I'm sorry, but you're not going on tonight—or tomorrow, for good measure. Wayne can do your part. He was okay last night." Wayne Collie was the understudy for the role.

"Suit yourself." If Malcolm was upset by the decision, he didn't show it. He looked tired, beat, and Fergie realized that Chris had been right. Those had been his own emotions Malcolm had been using up.

Chris dropped the wrist he held. He pressed Malcolm's shoulder as he turned away. "You were very good. Tops. Just get yourself all together for next week."

Monday, rehearsals for *Blythe Spirit* would go on in earnest—with Malcolm serving as stage manager for that production—and beginning Thursday, *Golden Boy* would be presented again.

Fergie followed Malcolm into the dressing room, where others of the cast were taking off their makeup or just lounging around talking over the performance: Peter; Norman; Ralph Mason, who played Roxy Gottlieb; Victor Smith, who played Tokio; the guy whose name he never remembered, who had the part of Mr. Carp. Had they all been checked out by Gene and found above suspicion in the matter of Maryellen's death? He supposed so. Certainly they had all left the theater that night before he had . . .

Victor Smith's eyes met his in the mirror, then switched to Mal's. "It went okay, eh, Malcolm?" Victor was a wizened little guy, the oldest member of the cast. He was a retired stockbroker.

"Yeh, fine. You were great, Victor."

Victor grinned and went on removing greasepaint. But he looked curiously again at Malcolm in the mirror. "Are the police breathing down your neck, Malcolm? On account of—"

"Not at the moment. But they'll be back." There was a bitter twist to his lips and violence in the gesture with which he threw a wad of Kleenex into the wastebasket.

"Don't worry, Mal," Fergie murmured. "They're concentrating on me, not you." He had spoken low, but at once the eyes of all those present turned to rest upon either him or his reflection—speculatively. He wished he had not called attention to himself.

"That's right, I wouldn't worry," agreed Victor Smith. "I'm sure if the police get anyone at all for this, it'll be the right man. So often with these sex crimes they never catch the guilty party." His eyes shifted from Malcolm to rest on Fergie.

Does he think I'm the right man? thought Fergie . . . the guilty party?

"Listen," he said to Mal, trying to sound nonchalant, as though his innocence could not possibly be in question, "come on up to the house for a drink."

"Fine." Malcolm seemed cheered by the suggestion.

"I'll wait for you outside." The dressing room was making him claustrophobic.

He joined Frank Wells and Peter Tarinelli, who were standing backstage talking.

Peter turned to Fergie. "Is Malcolm okay? I mean, how's he taking it that Chris won't let him go on?"

"I don't think he cares, one way or the other."

"That was some performance of his! I was afraid he was going to fly apart right on stage! Effective, though. The audience thought he was great—and so did I, since he pulled it off."

"A little unnerving for some of the rest of us!" Frank shook his head. "I kept thinking he was going to get carried away and adlib and miss a cue."

"Well, he didn't." Peter looked down at them both from his greater height and smoothed back his dark curly hair. "What did he mean," he asked Fergie, "by that remark about being Hamlet today?"

"Nothing much, I guess. Maybe that he feels ready to play Shakespeare. Look"—he glanced back and forth from Peter to Frank—"let's not rush the kid into a full-fledged nervous breakdown. He just needs a little time—to get over Maryellen's being murdered."

Yet even as he spoke he wondered how her death could have caused his young friend to give such a manic performance. He'd have thought it would act on him as a depressant.

Malcolm came out of the dressing room just then.

"Ready, Ferguson? I can certainly use that drink!"

Fergie went with him out to his car.

What a novel feeling to be taking a guest home. He hadn't invited anyone over, he realized, since his mother had died.

It wasn't till Saturday night that Gene Mack got around to checking on Malcolm Ludlow's account of his actions on the night Maryellen Polk had been killed. To be fair, he'd check it out. He wanted to be sure he was being fair to Ferguson Brady.

Ferguson had accused him of bias. "You dislike me," he'd said, when Gene had followed him out of police headquarters after all the questioning that morning. "And because you do, you're trying to pin a murder on me."

It was true that he didn't like Ferguson—snobbish dilettante sitting around with a private income and just doing what he wanted to, not even holding down a job. But it was also true—as the Chief agreed—that the evidence seemed to point to him. Queer duck—a recluse—and interested, though he tried to hide it, in young girls—very young girls.

"I'm only going by the evidence," he'd told Ferguson.

"Which you are twisting to suit yourself."

"I'm checking everyone out. Not just you." He had raked him with a look, which included the bicycle on which Ferguson had pedalled his way down to the station. Anyone who didn't even drive a car . . .

Hyslop had shook him up during the lengthy interrogation

—Ferguson had gotten plenty upset. But not enough to crack.

Well, naturally it wasn't going to be easy.

The music at the Anchor Chain, the bar Malcolm said he'd gone to after the *Golden Boy* opening, was enough to send you right out the door again. Loud, a lot of electronic effects. Live music—a group of five long-haired kids, one with a little goatee. Shapes, male and female, gyrated on the crowded dance floor, each doing his or her own thing with concentrated energy. The light in the place—what there was of it—looked gray from the cigarette smoke.

Gene had a glossy of Malcolm he'd picked up from the gal who was handling publicity for the theater group, Sally Sterns. She'd had a bunch of pictures of the *Golden Boy* cast.

"Yes, he's been in here," the bartender, a young man with a luxuriant auburn mustache and sideburns, told him when at last Gene had gotten his attention. "Haven't seen him tonight, though."

"When was he in?"

"Couple of times. Last week, this week."

"Do you remember what nights?"

"Not really. Two-three nights ago, I guess. Could have been Wednesday. Or Thursday."

"You're not sure?"

The bartender shook his head. "There's a lotta people in here every night. The best I can do is tell you it was the middle of the week some time. Not Friday—that was only yesterday, I'd remember. Could even have been Tuesday. Tuesday, Wednesday, or Thursday. Take your pick."

"You know a girl named Millie? Well-stacked blonde? Was in here the same night. She was with a fellow named

Guy—about six foot, bushy hair almost like an Afro, but he's white." Millie and Guy were two of the people Malcolm had hoped might remember him—if Gene could find them.

"I don't know the names. Doesn't mean they weren't here. But the descriptions would fit quite a few of the customers."

Gene could see that they might.

"How about a short, dark girl named Doris? Came with another girl—skinny, medium-colored hair, glasses?"

A shrug. "Lotta girls come together, in pairs. Not soliciting, you know. They're just kids, come for the music, and maybe they'll run into some boys they know, somebody that'll ask them to dance."

Gene stubbed a finger at the picture of Malcolm, which lay on the wet-ringed bar. "This man says he danced with the one named Doris. I'd like to locate her—or get her last name."

"I can't help you. Maybe one of the waiters will remember. But you know this place has only been open a couple of weeks. It's not like we've had time to collect a bunch of regulars."

Gene tried the waiters, of which there were two.

The first was no help. But the second gave him a bonus he hadn't even been looking for.

He was a hollow-cheeked youth with a weak chin and big, staring eyes. "Yes, I know him. But why you asking about him?" he asked sullenly. "He wouldn't kill nobody!"

Gene immediately wondered whether Malcolm had rehearsed the waiter on what to say.

"What makes you think he's suspected of killing anyone?"

"Why else would you be asking about him? Everyone knows a girl was murdered up at the theater where he's got the lead in a play."

"Did he talk to you about Maryellen Polk?"

"No." Sullenly, still. "I knew he was going to be in the play, that's all, and then I heard on the radio about some girl being killed after the first performance. No way Malcolm Ludlow'd do a thing like that!"

"Well, he hasn't been accused." This kid was the kind who called all police officers "pigs"—Gene could tell. "I'm just trying to check out what he told me."

The large eyes in the thin face looked up at him suspiciously; he waited, holding his round tray, empty, at his side.

"When was Mr. Ludlow last in here?" Gene asked.

There was a short pause while the waiter considered the question. He blinked and looked away, and Gene had time to regret that he'd told him anything at all, because now he was watching this cop-hater figure out what he should say to be of help to Malcolm.

The little waiter licked his lips. "It must have been Thursday night."

Damn! He should have started the questioning differently; then he'd have been sure this was the truth and not a friendly lie.

"The bartender thought it was Wednesday he was here. Wednesday night." Test him out a little.

"Wednesday? I don't think so. I remember it as Thursday." He was being careful, tentative. Either he really didn't remember, or it hadn't been Thursday at all.

"Who was he with? Do you remember the girl he was dancing with?"

"I didn't notice."

"She was sitting with him at the table. Didn't you wait on them?"

"It was a booth, not a table. And there was several people all crowded together. I didn't notice he even danced. I was busy."

"He says he danced with a short, dark girl named Doris. She came in with a skinny girl, medium-colored hair and glasses. You don't remember them?"

"No."

"Well then, do you remember what time Mr. Ludlow got here that night? And how long he stayed?"

"He was here quite a while. I think he stayed till we closed. Yeh, he did."

"But what time did he arrive?"

And Gene was sure now that the waiter was fabricating, because his dilemma showed in his gaunt face—he was looking for a *safe* lie: if the time he gave was too early, Malcolm couldn't have gotten here yet because he was still on stage in Chillingworth; too late, and the kid'd be doing his customer (and friend?) no good.

"I don't remember what time exactly he come in."

"You're sure though that it was Thursday? Not Wednesday?"

"Thursday."

"Sal!" The bartender called above the noise in the place to the waiter standing with Gene. Sal's eyes went to the row of drink orders lined up on the bar.

"I gotta go," he said. "They're waiting for their drinks."

"Just one more thing. You said Ludlow wouldn't kill anybody. Why'd you say that? You know him for quite a while?"

"Sure. I've waited on him lotta times."

"But I understood from the bartender that he's only been in a couple times. And this place has been open just about two weeks?"

Sal nodded. "I meant I'd waited on him before. Not here." He was edging away.

"Where was that? Where did you work before?"

But Sal was making his way to the end of the bar, where

his order of beers and highballs and tequila sunsets waited. He either didn't hear or didn't want to answer.

Gene squeezed through the crowd; he stood at Sal's elbow as the waiter transferred the glasses to his tray.

"I said where did you work before?"

Sal looked around at him with the same resentment he'd shown when Gene had first begun to question him. "At the Argonaut." He escaped with his tray.

The information struck Gene with all the reverberations of a clapper hitting the side of its bell.

A whole new angle. A whole new approach to this case.

The Argonaut was a gay bar.

TEN

Alice had tried several times on Saturday to call Ferguson. She'd tried in the morning and there had been no answer. Then she had driven down to Chillingworth Pharmacy and bought a copy each of *The Wilton Bulletin, The Westport News,* and *The Chillingworth Chronicle.* She'd taken them home, studied the "Pets for Sale" sections, and in the afternoon had again dialed Gus's number without success. She had wanted him to help her pick a dog. She had no intention of spending another night alone in the house.

It was Sunday morning now, and Chris Durham was looking skeptically at what she had bought.

"What is it?"

"A watchdog."

"Oh, I can *see* that!" The animal lay on its woolly back, all four feet in the air, wagging its tail against the floor boards and looking apprehensively at Chris out of the corner of one eye. "I mean what breed is it?"

"Mixed. The people I got him from said poodle and dachshund, but there's something else in there. Neither of those comes spotted." He was white with large liver-colored splotches. "His name's Poochie."

"Not much of a watchdog."

"He barks. That's all I wanted. I don't need an animal that's going to tear anyone limb from limb."

"Then you needn't worry." He snapped his fingers at the dog, and when it did not get up, he dropped dispiritedly into a chair.

"I'm being evicted," he said.

"Evicted? I thought you owned that house."

"I and the bank. Yes. But not for long. Not only is my wife asking for it as part of the divorce settlement; she is throwing me bodily out of it as of tomorrow."

"Too bad. That *is* kind of sudden."

"She and the kids are driving back from her mother's in Syracuse, and she wants me out."

"You don't have to go, you know. Even after you've filed for a divorce, you can go right on living under the same roof until the decree is final. Didn't your lawyer tell you that?"

"I don't have a lawyer. I'll have to find one."

Alice went back to work on the length of chintz she'd been hemming when he arrived. It was a floral pattern, with birds, which she'd bought for the living-room windows. "Anyway you don't have to get out of the house. Not at this point."

"You haven't met my wife." He watched her solemnly as she pulled needle and thread through the fabric. "Alice—I can count on you to hold my hand through this thing, can't I?"

"Literally or figuratively?"

"Both. I love you, Alice. I've tried to tell you that, and you wouldn't let me. You seem such a stickler about this marriage bit."

"Oh, that's only a pretext. The fact is you're like a rutting moose; you'll try to make any female that wanders into your territory. I've never wanted to be part of the herd, and I expect your wife doesn't like it much either."

He looked pained. "You didn't put that very nicely—or accurately. I don't know why girls always jump to the wrong conclusion about me. You, my wife, the girls in my drama classes . . ."

Alice smiled. "What about the girls in your classes?"

He spread his hands. "I don't know what comes over them. Maybe they think that's how show business is—fall in love with the director and you'll become a star. Maybe it's just ordinary pupil crushes on a teacher. I don't know. But Christ, Alice, I'm a victim, not a perpetrator!"

"You don't subscribe to the theory that everyone is really the architect of his own fate?"

"Hell, no. Though I'm trying. That's what I'm trying to do right now—run my life the way I want it. Which means having you, Alice. You're a mature enough person to see that these little college girls are simply silly kids trying out their emotions, and if you . . ."

She was grinning at him. "You don't *know*, Chris, that you come on like a slavering wolf? The first time you walked in here . . ."

He struck the arm of his chair with the flat of his hand. "It's menagerie time? I'm a moose, I'm a wolf . . ." He got up and before she realized what he was doing he had her by the wrist and on her feet. His arm went around her and he kissed her expertly, ending with a hand on her buttocks and his body pressed close against hers.

"How about it, Alice?" His eyes had a hungry look, and she wondered whether he'd heard about Clark Gable's rumored technique of thinking about a thick, juicy steak when he looked into his leading lady's eyes.

"That's very nice," she said. "Though I didn't need a

demonstration. I've never doubted that you're an expert."
She was thinking, maddeningly, of Gus leaning against her
car the other night in the parking lot, telling her he was
concerned about her. *Concerned*—yeh. And that was all.
They were friends, he'd said. Sure.

"This is not a demonstration. I'm trying to tell you I love
you!" He massaged her back, her hips, her thighs. "Will you
marry me, Alice, when I'm free?"

She put her hands on his shoulders and pushed him away.
"Thanks, but I couldn't possibly take your offer seriously.
You've known me less than three weeks and you're still
married."

"Later, then. You'll see—we'll be great together!"

She backed off, shaking her head. "I haven't said yes to
anything, so don't—"

"But you didn't say no, either."

She didn't like the smug, devilish look on his face.

"So I'll say no."

Would she be sorry, she wondered? After the year and a
half with Maury, she found that living alone did not have the
attraction for her she'd thought it would.

She sighed, a reaction Chris took for regret that she'd felt
she must turn him down at this stage of things. It was too
early to have asked her, that was all. There was lots of time
yet . . .

But the sigh had been for Ferguson Brady.

Ferguson was in his workshop on Sunday afternoon when
Gene Mack dropped in.

"Theater business? Or police business?" Fergie asked
when he looked up and saw the tall, sullen-faced policeman
ambling toward him.

"Police."

"Go right ahead. Sit down, if you'd like." He motioned to a chair he had just finished repairing for a friend of his mother's.

Gene shook his head and leaned against the end of the workbench. Fergie picked up a gouge and went back to the delicate job of removing the wood from around a design of acorns and oak leaves.

"You're pretty close to Malcolm, I've noticed."

"We've gotten to be friends. Yes."

"How'd that come about? You know him before you joined the theater group?"

"No. The day Chris brought the set drawings for me to see, Malcolm came along. He was so interested in the woodworking I do here that very shortly I started showing him how to do a few things. He seems to have quite a bit of talent along this line."

"But in addition to the woodworking, you've become very close—isn't that so?"

Fergie felt that he was being maneuvered, but toward what? "I'm not sure what you mean by 'close.' He's a likable kid, and since I've taken up with the theater company, we've spent some time together."

Gene's eyes narrowed as he looked at Fergie, and his squiggly eyebrows drew together. "You're a very careful person, aren't you, Ferguson. So careful you won't drive a car for fear you'll be in an accident. So careful about your private life—living all alone up here in the woods. You could be up to anything—anything at all—and who would know about it?"

Anger began to simmer somewhere in the region of Fergie's midriff. "Such as?" he asked.

"You're so careful there seems to be very little I can do to check on you. But your friend is *not* so careful. Malcolm

106

Ludlow—and I'm sure this is not news to you—is a thoroughgoing homosexual."

"He's *what?* Just how did you manage to fabricate that bit of—"

"No, it's true. I was checking Malcolm's alibi for the night Maryellen was killed—*being* fair to you, you see, and investigating everyone else I thought could have been involved. What I came across was that Malcolm is a frequenter of gay bars. Locally, the Argonaut. I've contacted the police in his home territory in Westchester and got their report this afternoon. Seems he's well known there as gay. That's why he doesn't live at home. His father threw him out."

And that's why he busted up with Maryellen, Fergie was thinking. Girls didn't work out for him.

He looked levelly at Gene. "You're a police officer. You wouldn't make up something like that, I know. But I'm willing to bet that not a single member of the Chillingworth Theatre group knew this about Malcolm. And that includes Maryellen; she didn't know he was anything but straight. Maybe he's been trying to make it as a heterosexual since he moved here."

Gene smiled and shook his head. "If that's so would he be going to a place like the Argonaut? He's been a regular there up until three or four weeks ago. That's about when he met you . . ."

Fergie felt as though a giant fissure had opened in the ground at his feet. At the bottom of it was . . . God knew what. He felt cold and sick.

"There's nothing like that between Malcolm and me! Between me and anybody! Nothing! And there never was."

"I don't believe you. You and Malcolm became lovers at some point. Maybe he was trying, as you suggested, to make it as a heterosexual—with Maryellen. But it didn't work out.

He broke up with her because of you. Then something went wrong between you. The night the play opened, there they were together backstage, Malcolm and Maryellen—patching it up. Or so it appeared. You believed she had come between you and Malcolm—and that's why you killed her."

His mind had cleared. "And raped her?" he asked coldly. Mack had no basis for any of this. It was only the complete unexpectedness of his accusation that had thrown Fergie off balance. "If I were so hot for boys, I'm sure Maryellen wouldn't have turned me on at all."

"AC-DC, as they say. I hear some people like both."

"And some people are bastards." His temper was boiling by now and he glared at Gene Mack.

Gene chose to ignore the insult. "Besides, we've no proof of actual rape. Molestation—yes. That was quite evident. But the Polks withdrew their initial consent to an autopsy. We don't know whether her killer actually—"

Ferguson went on with his woodworking, willing his hands not to shake in anger. "Have you accosted Malcolm —you don't mind my choice of words, I hope?—on this subject of his preferences?"

"No. I haven't been able to find him. You wouldn't know where he might be?"

"No. Though if I did I wouldn't tell you. I can only assure you he's neither under my bed nor in it."

Gene turned away. "Well, thanks for the cooperation," he said unpleasantly.

"You vary your theories but not your suspect," Fergie stated to the other's retreating back. "You've measured me for this crime, and you're going to fit it to me no matter what. *Aren't you?*"

Gene turned to face him. "I'm being perfectly fair. I'm bending over backwards trying to be fair! But it's a fact I

108

don't like your kind, and if I can cut you down I will."

In three strides Fergie caught up with him—faced him, heart pounding in fury. "What do you mean by 'my kind'?"

Gene smiled a little contemptuously. "Want to be arrested for striking an officer?" He nodded at Fergie's clenched right fist. "Your kind," he said thoughtfully. "Well, that's what I'm trying to prove, isn't it. I hope the question will be fully answered in court."

He turned on his heel and went out.

The phone was ringing when Ferguson went into the house through the back door, into the kitchen. It was nearly five, he saw by the old wall clock with its painted scene of a mountain sunset. He'd worked like a demon after Mack left and had lost all track of time.

He picked up the receiver.

"Gus, where have you been? I've been phoning and phoning."

"I was in my workshop. How are you, Alice?"

"Impatient. I was hoping you could come to dinner. And I'd nearly given up."

"Don't give up—I'll come. When?"

"Now. Shall I come over and fetch you?"

"No. I can get there under my own power. This isn't a party, is it?"

"No. Just you and me."

He showered and shaved, regretting the time spent when it would take him so long, as it was, to get to Alice's.

It wasn't the first time he'd felt irked recently that he didn't drive. In his haste he almost forgot to feed Monty and the cats. He came back in the house, dished out the dog's food and put it down for him, then opened two cans of liver and gravy, which he divided among four saucers out on the porch. Then he was able to take off.

Downhill; a mile or so on the level; past the town hall and the school; past the drugstore and the grocery; across the tracks.

He imagined himself already there and pedalled faster. Uphill, down and up again. At last he coasted into Alice's drive and parked his bike beside the walk.

What a wonderful feeling it was to have someone waiting for him!

Someone was, indeed—and barking.

As he reached the front stoop the barking rose to a crescendo. Alice opened the door and said, "Come in." The dog was peering out at him from behind her long skirt.

"Hi," he said to it. Alice stepped aside and he had a glimpse, before it collapsed onto its back, of a woolly, low-slung animal something like an attenuated sheep with spots.

"This is Poochie."

"Likely to take my leg off, I can see." He leaned over and patted the writhing stomach. "Some exotic Italian breed?"

"Oh, no. Not Pucci as in scarf. Spelled as in *dog*. He came with the name and I don't think he's up to having it changed. You know, I tried all day yesterday to get hold of you. I decided to get a dog for protection and I wanted you to help me pick one out."

"This was advertised as a dog?"

"Oh, he's fine. I've become very attached to him."

She was startlingly beautiful this evening. Her eyes looked larger, darker, the lashes longer than ever. She was wearing an ankle-length flowered garment in reds and blues, slit up the side to about her thigh, and she was barelegged. There was also a slit down the front to her waist and it made him quite nervous.

She poured them each a Scotch in the kitchen and took

him out to the brick terrace behind the living room, in the angle between the old section of the house and the newer part that had been added at the back. Here they overlooked the river, a hundred feet below at the bottom of the hill.

"Why don't you trade in the dog—on a larger model that stands on its own four feet?" It had taken refuge under the bench on which she sat and seemed to be smiling at him, with its lips drawn back and the corners of its mouth turned up.

"No, I only want him to make noise—and for company."

"After what's happened it's a good idea, I guess—a dog. When you're all alone here." Though he had never thought of Alice as a girl who would be afraid of anything.

"They haven't arrested anyone yet?" she asked.

"No. They're still investigating."

"Chris is sure it was someone who just happened to be at the barn that night—someone they'll never be able to trace. Anyone could have bought a ticket; someone from miles away . . ."

"Chris *would* favor a theory that would let him out."

"Oh, Gus! Really! Just because you don't happen to like Chris—"

"Where was he when it happened, by the way? I suppose he's got some great alibi."

"No, he doesn't have. He left before all of the cast had gone—went down to Wilton to deposit the box office receipts in the night depository at the bank. After that he went home and to bed, but he has no one to corroborate that that's where he was—or what time he got there."

"And he'd have to have driven past the barn again on his way home. How long does it take to get to that bank and back to Chillingworth Center again? Ten minutes each way? So less than twenty minutes after he left the theater he was cruising by it again—about the time everyone would have

111

gone—and there'd have been only Maryellen left, looking for her sweater in the dark. And her car parked where Chris could have seen it."

She was angry. "Chris isn't like that! Sure, he thinks he's a devil with women, but he's harmless really. He was fond of Maryellen, as you'd be fond of a—of a child. He'd never have hurt her in any way."

"How do you know? You've never even seen them together, as far as I know."

"He told me. And I believe him. Because I know what he's like. Personally, I still favor Frank Wells as a suspect. He waited on me when I was in the drugstore yesterday. That's one hell of a deep scratch on his cheek! And doesn't it seem an awfully convenient coincidence that the night of the opening just happened to be the time a bunch of horses got loose in his yard?"

"He's got a witness. Burton Sayles helped him catch the horses. Frank was worried, I know. He was sure the police would suspect him because of his face being scratched. But he was saying yesterday, at the matinee, that he's completely in the clear now. Burton had been watching television and could pinpoint the time at which he got home. And Frank was kept busy long enough after that, so that he couldn't have been involved with Maryellen."

"Well, that's nice. How about your friend Malcolm? Does he turn out to have an alibi?"

Fergie took a swallow of his drink. "Maybe. Or maybe not. He went down to some bar on the Post Road after the performance. Who knows whether anyone can back him up on what time he got there."

He didn't feel like telling her about the homosexual business. He was too upset by it.

But Alice had noted the change of expression on his face.

112

"What's wrong, Gus?"

"Same thing that's been wrong ever since Maryellen was killed. Gene Mack's doing everything he can to pin her murder on me."

"He can't do that without evidence."

"Then he'll get me tarred and feathered and run out of town. He doesn't like me."

"What makes you think that?"

"It's been obvious." He explained how they had failed to hit it off from the beginning of their working together on the sets.

"Well," she said, "but even if his nose was a little out of joint—and granted that you seem to rub each other the wrong way—that's no basis for his trying to frame you for rape and murder."

"I didn't say 'frame.' He's an honest cop—he wouldn't do a thing like that. What I mean is that he looks at the evidence and at my past history with the preconceived conviction that I'm guilty. That's what's so scary, Alice. He believes, absolutely believes, that I did it."

He turned away to stare down at the narrow river at the bottom of the hill, its riffling brown water just visible beyond the trunks of the trees that grew on the steep slope. When he wasn't looking at Alice it was easier to talk to her. He could almost convince himself that somewhere, hidden away beneath her glamorous exterior, there was still the plain, drab, no-nonsense girl she had once been.

"What's so awful," he went on, "is that when I try to see myself as Gene Mack must, his theories fit damnably well. A recluse . . . secretive . . . I don't date girls. I'm so queer I don't even drive a car. A freak." He grimaced.

"Oh, Gus, stop it!" She reached over and put her hand on his arm. "You're a perfectly normal guy—as anyone ought

113

to be able to see—but a very private person. And the recluse business—that's just circumstances, really." She removed her hand, but its warm imprint stayed on, an invisible benison. "You were in a rut for a while, with no one locally to talk to, but that's over. You've been active in the theater group, you've been running all over the place with me—"

"Oh, but Alice. That's just it. Such a change isn't credible! Not to the police; not to Gene, certainly. Yesterday Chief Hyslop had me at the police station grilling me, with Gene standing by. They've been over my whole past history with a microscope and have decided I'm exactly the type they're looking for."

"What do you mean by 'whole past history'? You haven't a police record . . ."

"No. What they've got now I suppose they'd call a profile. The Chief went on and on about how I've been interested only in very young girls—you, for instance"—his voice cracked—"when you were fourteen and I was twenty-one. Sharon Kelsey when she was fifteen and I was nineteen. I tried to say that there wasn't much of an age difference there, but Hyslop's point was that I never *had* been interested in anything older than a pubescent girl. Most recently Maryellen, of course. He accused me of killing Maryellen because I thought she'd gone back to Malcolm."

The newer accusation he couldn't bring himself to tell her—that he'd been Malcolm's lover and Maryellen had gotten in the way.

"Accused you, but didn't charge you. There's quite a difference. They're hassling you, hoping that if you're guilty you'll break. They're probably using the same treatment on some of the others."

"But Gene Mack's the officer in charge of the case, and he's concentrating on me."

114

Once again she reached out to him and put her hand on his. "Don't worry, Gus. You'll be all right. And if you want to change your profile, you can start dating me anytime. I'm twenty-five now—hardly a pubescent girl."

"Thanks, Alice." She thought his eyes lit up for a moment, but then the look in them changed and he said sardonically, "You think I can ride you on the handlebars of my bike?"

She didn't know whether he was putting himself down or rejecting her offer because he'd taken it for charity. But she didn't think this was the time to try to find out.

She refilled his drink.

The mosquitoes drove them in, and they had dinner in the stone-floored room off the kitchen, which had once been a sort of service and storeroom. Alice had fixed it up with wicker chairs and a table and decorated it with pots of greenery and hanging baskets of geraniums.

"This is nice," Fergie said.

"I got the furniture at a garage sale. Had to beat off several other buyers. It's great, isn't it? At this point I don't need a formal dining room—and couldn't afford it anyhow."

There were three blue Japanese lanterns suspended from hooks in the wooden ceiling. Alice lit the candles in them, and the ones in glass holders on the table. There was a blue cloth on the table, and a bowl of petunias.

He tried to remember when he'd last eaten at a table with a cloth on it. At Leona's on Thanksgiving, of course; and he'd had lunch in New York sometime in the spring, at the Oak Room in the Plaza—he liked occasionally to go to one of the good restaurants in town. Not out here, though—he'd have felt conspicuous. In the suburbs or in the country, people dined out in pairs or groups.

They had coq au vin, rice with fresh peas, and spinach

salad. Fergie had seconds of them all. And then there were strawberries heaped on ice cream.

He helped her clear the table, blew out the candles, and they put the dishes in the dishwasher. Then they had coffee in the living room.

As they sat on either side of the fireplace in chairs that had been Fergie's, Alice looked around at the sparse furnishings of the room—the cobbler's bench, the pair of rush stools that didn't match, the maple love seat under which Poochie had taken refuge, the little end table that was holding up a lamp too big for it. "I'm not sure what I think I'm doing with this place. Camping out, it looks like." She gestured at the rugless floor and at the windows, only one of which had curtains.

"Sorry you came?"

"Oh, no."

"You don't regret leaving what's-his-name?" He didn't know why he'd asked—the question had just popped out. And he didn't really want to hear the answer.

"Maury. Definitely not."

"I'd have thought you might have ended up marrying him."

"I'd have thought so, too, before we lived together. I do believe in making a commitment to another person, but by now I'm not so sure about marriage. It seems to me more like a strait jacket than anything else."

So that was how Maury what's-his-name had affected her? He felt unexpectedly relieved. For some reason Fergie had taken a great dislike to this man Alice had lived with. He must surely have put undue pressure on her, taken advantage of her . . .

Poochie emerged suddenly woofing from under the love seat, as the beam of a car's headlights flashed across the front

116

windows, and Fergie had a prevision of Maury arriving at the door to fetch Alice back to the city.

But it was Chris who opened the door, even before Alice reached it, and stepped into the hallway.

"Oh." Chris's eyes rounded in surprise. "I didn't know you had company. No car out front . . ."

"Gus was here to dinner."

And Fergie didn't like the way Durham had come in without being asked. He had knocked, but still . . .

"How are you, Ferguson?" Chris slouched into the living room and took possession of the love seat. Poochie crawled under Alice's chair. "I just thought I'd stop in," he went on to Alice, "and see how you and Fido were making it."

"Fine. He's a good barker."

"I heard. Lotta protection . . ." He eyed the dog, who stared back at him from under a fold of her skirt.

"Do you happen to have seen Malcolm around?" he asked Ferguson. (Did *everyone* have him linked now with Mal? Damon and Pythias; Dorian Gray and—)

"Not today," he said curtly. "The only person I've seen besides Alice was Gene Mack."

"Oh. He talk to you about the new set?"

"No. Police business."

"Ah." Chris frowned and looked hastily away, and Fergie was glad to see that mention of police activity had made him uneasy. Maybe Alice was right—the cops were giving all of them a bad time.

Chris was lacing and unlacing his fingers. "I've moved up rehearsal time for tomorrow evening—for *Blythe Spirit.* I wanted to get hold of Malcolm to tell him, but I can't raise him on the phone."

Mack hadn't been able to find him either, Fergie remem-

117

bered, and remembered also what a strange, almost desperate mood Mal had been in yesterday when he had come over for drinks. He had worried about him after he had gone, and he was aware now of a vague stirring of apprehension.

"If you hear from him," Chris said, "would you tell him rehearsal's at seven-thirty instead of eight?"

"You can reach him at work tomorrow—at the bank." He didn't feel like carrying messages for Chris Durham.

"Oh, sure. I can, at that."

Alice had gotten another cup and poured Chris some coffee. How long was he going to stay? wondered Fergie. He would outstay him.

They discussed the set for the new play. ("You know, Ferguson, we're going to *have* to build it up in your workshop. There's no other place." "Well, I'll see . . .")

Alice inquired of Chris when did he expect his family to arrive on the morrow.

Chris inquired of Fergie whether he knew of any bachelor lodgings in the area to which he could move.

Fergie said they were hard to find.

Chris turned over the matter of Maryellen's funeral in the morning. Yes, he was going—it was the least he could do.

Fergie asked Chris how he thought the police investigation was going.

Chris said he didn't know.

Alice finally shooed both of them out.

"Can I give you a lift home?" Chris offered as they went down the flagstone walk.

"No, thanks," Fergie said stiffly. "I've got a light on my bike."

118

Touchy bastard, Chris thought as he got into his car and started the engine.

Goddamn condescending, Fergie remarked to himself, feeling as if his manhood had been attacked.

He got on his bike, pedalled out the drive before Chris had finished backing to turn around, and a moment later coasted down the hill.

ELEVEN

At about eight-thirty-five on Monday morning, Gene Mack, in his blue and white Chillingworth police car, pulled into Mrs. Seide's driveway.

Malcolm Ludlow's green Mustang was parked, he found, as it had been yesterday, on the black asphalt at the bottom of the steps leading up the slight incline to the studio apartment where he lived.

Good. He'd caught him before he left for work.

There was neither bell nor knocker for the door, so Gene rapped on the panels with his knuckles.

He waited, while two bluejays shrilled and scolded in the apple tree at the corner by the woodpile, and a wasp or bee of some kind buzzed by, but nothing happened.

He pounded hard on the door, waited, and pounded again. Then he walked around the corner to the big window and peered through the same gap in the drapes that had been there yesterday when he'd checked the studio, looking for Malcolm. (And had concluded that *Golden Boy*'s young lead must have spent the night elsewhere and was not back yet.)

120

The bed was still unmade. (As it had been yesterday.) No one lay in it.

A wave of disappointment mingled with annoyance and the beginnings of baffled anger swept over him. It had been Malcolm Ludlow who had raped and killed Maryellen? Malcolm Ludlow all along, and not Ferguson Brady? And he'd been wasting his time and the opportunity of solving the crime with resultant personal glory and chance of promotion? Because Malcolm was gone. Fled. Leaving his car parked where it would deceive anyone looking for him into believing that he was still here.

Gene walked all around the studio, listening for any sound from within—such as that of the shower, which might have prevented his quarry from hearing the knocking on his door. He heard nothing except the same bluejays and the sound of a car going by on the road.

"Damn! God damn!"

Fortunately Mrs. Seide was at home. She was eating breakfast in the kitchen when he came to the side door of the gray clapboard house—he caught sight of her through the window, peering out at him with a glass of tomato juice in her hand.

"Good morning, Officer." When she appeared in a flowered wrapper at the screen door she had left her juice behind and was hastily smoothing her unkempt brown-dyed hair with both hands. She hadn't yet combed it—and was embarrassed, he guessed, that anyone should have caught her without her makeup on. That she usually wore makeup was attested to by the smudges of mascara on the puffy places under her eyes—it had come off during the night.

"Mrs. Seide?" He knew her name because it was on the mailbox. But he knew it also because the fame of her late husband, Bernard Seide, still lingered on locally, causing the Seide place to be pointed out as a Chillingworth landmark. "I'm trying to locate Malcolm Ludlow."

"Oh." She looked out past him in the direction of the studio. "Well, he must still be in the apartment. His car's there."

"I don't think he's home. There was no answer when I knocked."

"Oh, there wasn't?" She pulled at the straggly ends of her hair, trying to put it into better shape, and tightened the sash of her wrapper.

"When did you see him last?"

"When did I see him last . . ." She ran her fingers over her forehead and then thoughtfully down over a creased and wrinkled cheek. "I don't know. I never see much of him. But his car was there all day yesterday. At least I think it was. Oh, yes—I remember when I saw him last. It was on Friday afternoon. He was going up the walk to the studio, and I went out to ask him about that girl being killed. I'd heard about it when I went to the grocery."

"What did he say?"

"Not much. He looked upset and didn't seem to want to talk about it. I heard since then that he'd been dating her— the Polk girl. I hadn't known that. So no wonder he was upset. I suppose that's why he stayed home all day yesterday. Didn't feel like going out."

"But you didn't see him yesterday? Out in the yard or? . . ."

"No. He might have gone in or out and I wouldn't know, of course. I don't spend my time looking out of the windows except at the back, where I watch the birds at the birdbath."

"Do you have a key to the apartment, Mrs. Seide?"

"Certainly I have a key."

"Then I wonder if you could let me in over there."

Her face darkened into a scowl. "Why?"

"Because I want to find out why he doesn't answer the door."

"Oh." The scowl was replaced first by a blank look, then one of alarm. "Oh, you don't think? . . ." She put her hand to her mouth. "You don't think he could have . . . done something to himself?"

He didn't think so at all. But the conclusion to which Mrs. Seide had jumped saved his possibly having to argue with her over the fact that he hadn't a search warrant. "Could you get the key, Mrs. Seide?"

She fetched it from somewhere in the kitchen, and together they crossed her driveway and the stretch of grass beyond, ducked under the branches of the apple tree, and stepped onto the flagstone path.

Gene knocked again at the door, and when there was no answer after a few moments, motioned to her to use her key.

With trembling fingers she inserted it in the lock—the kind that was centered in the doorknob. The knob turned, but the door did not open when she pushed on it.

Mrs. Seide turned to him with wide eyes of which the whites, he noted, were a little yellow. "It's bolted from inside."

At her words his gut drew together with a sort of crawling sensation, and he felt a tightening in the muscles of his neck. The number of times during his twelve years as a police officer that he'd had to cope with a man armed with a gun could have been counted on the fingers of one hand. Yet this was just the kind of eventuality he'd been trained for.

He stepped to one side of the door and pulled Mrs. Seide after him. With a feeling of elation he unsnapped his holster and drew the .357 magnum he carried.

"You'd better go back in the house, Mrs. Seide. And stay out of the way of any firing there may be."

The sculptor's widow looked at him through narrowed lids. "You didn't say you thought he was a killer. You led me to believe you were afraid he might have tried to do away with himself." Her voice held anger and contempt. She apparently felt he had tricked her.

"*You* said he might have harmed himself; I didn't. I only said I wanted to know why he didn't answer the door."

"But you let me believe . . ." She pressed her colorless lips together. "You're mistaken, Officer. That boy didn't kill her. He—"

"Mrs. Seide, you're to do what I say. I'm going in there. And I want you out of the way. He may be armed."

She didn't move. But when he started to take hold of her, she retreated, backing up till she was at the corner of the studio.

"You stay there," he ordered. "And if there's any trouble, you get around the corner—immediately." He gave his attention again to the door. Standing next to it, with his back to the wall, he turned his head and called out. "Malcolm! This is Gene Mack. I'm armed, and I'm waiting. Unbolt this door and come out of there! Slowly, with your hands up . . .

"Do you hear me?"

"He doesn't hear you," Mrs. Seide said annoyingly. "And you look pretty silly, do you know that?"

He paid no attention to her. "Malcolm, are you in there?"

Still there was no sound from within. He got set for a run at the door, and as he started toward it, shoulder hunched to take the impact, he was only peripherally aware of the voice calling from beyond the apple tree, "Malcolm, he's coming in!"

The door banged in, the hardware of the bolt fastener

124

splintered from the doorframe. Gene's glance swept the room in one motion. There was no one in it—unless he was under the bed, which seemed unlikely. He strode across the room and flung open a door. Clothes closet. No one hiding there. Slowly he opened the other door, which swung in. Had to be the bathroom.

He felt the skin of his scalp move backward, and a sickness rose up in his throat.

Malcolm, clad in blue silk pajamas, was sitting in the glass shower stall. The upper part of his body was slumped over his bent knees, and his hands rested between his ankles. Gene stepped to the door of the shower for a better look. Malcolm had cut his wrists. The razor blade lay on the tile floor, near the drain.

"Oh, my God!" said Mrs. Seide from the doorway behind Gene.

Chief Hyslop turned away from inspecting the body in the shower stall. The sober set of his face was contradicted by the pleased and eager gleam in his blue eyes.

"Too bad, of course," he said to Gene Mack. "But good luck for us just the same. This certainly closes our murder case—and fast."

"Looks that way. Murder and suicide." Though Gene felt a bit disconsolate to find the case of which he'd been in charge solved in a manner he had not foreseen and with an explanation opposite to the one he'd been backing. He was left with all those dark suspicions of Ferguson Brady now—and with nothing to hang them on.

They photographed the body and also the splintered door frame, while they waited for the county detective from the state's attorney's office in Bridgeport and for the medical examiner. They photographed as well the nearly empty half-gallon bottle of Early Times that stood open on the night table.

"Must have primed himself for the act," said Chief Hyslop.

They inspected all the window locks from inside and then walked around the outside of the studio, a snug, attractive little place dominated by the huge stone chimney at one end. There was nothing amiss.

By the chimney they paused and looked down at the low door, a two-by-three-foot rectangle sawed right through the clapboards and set on hinges. A rusty padlock dangled open from the hasp-type fastener.

"Woodbox for the fireplace," said Chief Hyslop, eying the sprinkle of wood chips and crumbled bark on the ground between the little door and the stack of split logs at the corner of the building.

Gene knelt and removed the padlock, opened the door.

"Yeh, full of logs." He closed it.

Hyslop shrugged. "Well, anyhow it's a suicide, so . . ." He turned to glance over his shoulder at the driveway below. "Here's the doc."

Since time immemorial Dr. Clancy had been the local medical examiner. No one else wanted the job. He was a tall, rawboned man, white-haired, and carried himself erect.

"Hello, Jim." He lifted a hand as he came up the steps. "You've got a suicide as I hear it?"

"How are you, Jack? Yeh, go look. In the bathroom."

They loafed through the door in his wake. No use crowding him at his work.

But Doc Clancy was back with them in a matter of seconds.

"I hope you fellas have been busy fingerprinting in there. That's no suicide!"

126

They stared at him.

"But he slashed his wrists . . ." Hyslop said feebly.

Doc Clancy tilted his head back to look down at him through the bottom of his bifocals, as though examining Chillingworth's chief of police for some evidence of intelligence.

"Come and look. Not enough blood. They don't bleed, you know, when they're dead. This boy was dead when his wrists were cut. He was murdered."

Chris didn't like funerals. He loathed them, in fact. But it wouldn't look right if he didn't go to this one. After all, he was head of the theater group. And when he had talked to Maryellen's parents . . .

It hadn't helped either that the news about Malcolm had broken that morning. Gene Mack had come by as Chris was going out the door to drive up to the Sayles Funeral Home.

At least they seemed to be putting Malcolm's death down as suicide—or was that only a ploy to put him off his guard while they asked him about Malcolm? And possibly more about Maryellen? If the fuzz really thought, of course, that it was suicide, and assumed then that Malcolm had killed Maryellen, he himself had nothing more to worry about.

He had been living all this time in terror that Gene Mack or someone else on the force would go up to Dumont College to ask around about him, about his character and background and so forth. Or would even just make a phone call. And would find out that he was not employed there anymore. That the university had not renewed his contract—and why.

So far the police hadn't checked. At least he thought not, or they'd have been down on him like a ton of bricks.

Gene had had too much else to get through today, with the

discovery of another body, to ask him more than a few questions—about Malcolm, not Maryellen.

"No, I haven't seen him since the Saturday matinee. That was when I told him not to show up for the performance that night; his understudy could go on."

"Did he ask to be excused from the Saturday night show?"

"No. I told him he was in no shape to go on."

"Why not?"

He shrugged. "Anyone could see—anyone who'd watched him from close up during the matinee performance—that his nerves were absolutely shot. He was on the ragged edge."

"Edge of what? Some kind of breakdown? Ready to kill himself, would you say?"

"How do *I* know? Kill himself? Who ever knows when someone's ready to do something like that? Unless they say so? And you can't be sure even then."

"He didn't say anything to you that might have indicated he was contemplating suicide?"

"Hell, no. If he had, I'd have held his hand myself till he felt better. As it happened, I guess Ferguson did that. He invited Malcolm up to his house for a drink. And that's the last I saw of Malcolm. Poor kid!"

"Ferguson Brady. Hmm." And Chris saw that he had succeeded in deflecting Gene's interest from himself to another line of speculation.

Chris signed his name in the book laid out for the purpose on a polished table just outside the room where the service was to be held. Already there was quite a crush of people, many of them young, and he assumed these were members of Maryellen's graduating class at the high school. He found a seat at the back, nodding somberly to Lucy Cannon and Marta Guild nearby, and looked around to see who else was

128

there from the Chillingworth Theatre group. Quite a few. There was Frank, with his wife, near the front. And Victor Smith. Wayne Collie. And sitting in a group, a number of the kids who had worked with Maryellen on painting the flats. No sign of Ferguson.

The coffin was closed, thank goodness, with a blanket of pink roses over it. Quantities of flowers everywhere.

He wondered whether the police had sent a man to watch the mourners, in hopes that the killer would be among them and would betray himself in some manner that he could not foresee—or was that sort of thing done only in detective stories? He doubted, anyway, that the Chillingworth police force had a man to spare for such a detail.

He managed to block out most of the service because he was concentrating throughout on the problem of where he was going to live, what with Felicity returning and demanding that he move out of the house. He had first thought of pitching a tent in the back yard, a move that would suitably dramatize his plight and guarantee him the sympathy of friends. But the trouble was that he could hardly dig a latrine for himself out there, and so the idea wasn't really practical. With regret he relinquished his fantasies of grilling steaks on the portable barbecue right under Felicity's nose and throwing great parties under her windows—to which she was not invited.

Now he was into his next plan, which was to move into the theater. He could unroll his sleeping bag on the floor of the set, of nights, and in the daytime he could entertain Alice there, between rehearsals and performances, and Felicity would hear of it and realize that he was having a better time than he ever had at home. And then . . .

But the service was over. The coffin was wheeled past, the grieving family was shepherded out behind it, and there he was then, talking with Frank Wells under the front portico, with its immaculate white columns, while they waited for the burial procession to get under way.

"You heard about Malcolm?" Chris said to Frank, while Leona Wells talked in a low voice to an elderly woman with tears running down her face.

"Yes. Someone phoned Leona about it just before we left the house. Neighbor of Mrs. Seide's. I could hardly believe it!" Frank shook his head. "What happened? Do you know? Thelma could tell us very little . . ."

"He'd been dead for some time, I think—from what Gene said. It didn't just happen today. They only found him this morning, though. Suicide. He'd slashed his wrists."

"My goodness!" Frank was silent for a few moments while he contemplated this new tragedy, and then he said, "He was so strange during that last performance, remember?"

"Yes, he was. That was why I ordered him not to go on for the evening performance."

"I was relieved that you did. Though if any of us had realized he was *that* unstrung . . . I wonder when—?"

"I don't think they know for sure yet when he did it."

There. There was the one policeman who had come to the funeral. He had just arrived and was getting out of his official car right by the entrance gates. The funeral director—Mr. Sayles himself, Chris guessed from the manner in which he had silently marshalled and commanded his helpers during the service—nodded to the cop across the intervening area of paved driveway and returned to his orchestrating of the final notes of this ceremony of departure.

A minute later Mr. Sayles turned in surprise and annoyance as he discovered the cop right behind him instead of out in the road halting traffic as he was obviously supposed to be doing, so that the cortege could emerge onto the highway.

Chris could not hear what it was the policeman had come over to say, but it was a brief exchange. Then the officer strode back across the driveway and out to take up a position in the road, where he held up a hand, like Moses parting the waters, bringing traffic to a stop. The hearse pulled out and the black limousines followed it, with a string of private cars, lights on, behind them.

It was only by chance that Chris looked full into the handsome face of the funeral director as he walked up the steps past him. It was ashen, and in the man's eyes was a look of hell uncovered.

Chris was taken aback. He almost reached out a hand in assistance but instantly thought, why? It's *his* job, not mine, to lend succor to people. And what was wrong with him, anyway?

As Burton Sayles made in desperation for his office, where he could take refuge, he did not know that Chris Durham had watched him falter as he passed into the great, pretentious edifice his father had built—and that Chris had wondered why.

The gloom at police headquarters was knee deep.

There had been *some* blood from the wrists, of course (Hyslop and Mack weren't completely stupid, after all), but not enough.

Although it would probably be a week before the autopsy results came back—possibly giving the actual cause of death, possibly not—in the meantime there was the information obtained late that morning from Mrs. Seide's cleaning woman, Theodora Swanzey (who owned five rental properties in Danbury, drove a Cadillac and spent her winters in Florida), that last week the woodbox in the studio apartment had been nearly empty. And who, in a hot June, would have filled it with logs for a hypothetical autumn fire?

But someone wishing to camouflage the unusual exit by which he had left the studio . . .

These findings in the Malcolm Ludlow case Chief Hyslop was keeping, for the present, strictly under wraps.

He rode as though pursued by fiends. This time—this second interrogation at police headquarters—had been even more horrible than the first.

"No. I haven't seen Malcolm since Saturday."

"When Saturday?"

"A little after six. I asked him up to the house, after the matinee, for a couple of drinks."

It was Chief Hyslop asking the questions, the same as last time; with Gene Mack standing by. "You didn't go with him when he left your place? To his apartment?"

"No. Why would I do that?" It seemed to Fergie that there was something sly about the glances the other two exchanged.

"What *about* Malcolm?" he asked them, an uneasy premonition firming up rapidly, as he considered the kind of questions they were asking him. "Has something happened to him?"

"Don't you know?" Hyslop carefully asked, leaning forward a little from behind his desk and fixing him with bloodshot blue eyes.

"No, I don't know. But from the way your questions are slanted . . ." He waited for them to tell him.

"We found him in the shower at his apartment," Gene Mack said. "With his wrists slashed. He'd been dead for some time."

"Oh." Fergie felt the contraction of his brows in a frown of pity. And in just that second Malcolm's face and Chad's

132

face fused in his mind's eye, and he experienced all over again the sense of loss and the dreadful feeling of guilt that were more than a decade old.

Both police officers were studying him, hard-eyed, like two scientists examining a specimen wriggling on a pin.

Why? Why were they so interested in his reactions? If Malcolm had committed suicide, then—

Maybe it hadn't really *been* suicide.

He had a vision of Malcolm bleeding onto the tiles of his shower and was filled with a sense of outrage. "What a rotten thing to happen!" Some of Mal's odd, disturbed discourse from Saturday evening threaded its way into his consciousness that the Golden Boy was dead. What had he meant by all those obscure remarks?

It seemed suddenly important to know exactly how Mal had died. He appealed not to Mack, but to Hyslop. "Tell me about it. Please."

"No. You tell *me*. Everything you know about Ludlow's death."

Ferguson's jaw clenched. The man might as well have taken him by the scruff of the neck. "I don't know anything about it—except what Gene just told me."

"We believe Mr. Ludlow died Saturday night. And you don't know anything about it? He was at your house having drinks with you that afternoon and on into the evening—"

All right, he'd try to keep calm and tell them what he could. "Malcolm had been upset because the police were breathing down his neck. But it was something else that was bothering him Saturday. We'd talked before about Maryellen, about the police investigation. But something must have happened after our earlier conversation—which was on Friday, I guess. Yes, Friday. At that time he'd been mostly concerned about proving he hadn't even been near her when she died. But Saturday when he was at my house, he was talking about how dreadful it could be to have your hands tied because of a responsibility to someone else. And he seemed so angry."

"Angry at whom? About what?"

"When I asked him, he smiled in a funny way, kind of bitter, and said, 'Oh, never mind me. I'm just running off at the mouth.' " Ferguson turned to Gene. "It occurred to me at the time that maybe he had found out who raped and killed Maryellen, but that he wasn't free to talk. I asked him straight out, but he denied it."

"Have you come to any conclusion about why he died?"

"Maybe whoever strangled Maryellen killed him because Malcolm knew what he'd done."

Gene looked pleased. "Where did you get the idea that Malcolm was murdered?"

"It's a guess." His eyes narrowed. "Was he?"

It was Hyslop who answered. "Possibly."

"I suggest," said Gene, leaning against the wall and looking down at Ferguson, "that if Malcolm did 'run off at the mouth,' what he said scared you. You decided he was likely to talk to someone else in the same way and implicate you. Because *you* had killed Maryellen Polk. So you went home with Malcolm and staged an apparent suicide."

"No." He kept the lid on his temper. He must.

"Either that or you killed him in a rage when he rejected your advances after you'd gone home with him. And you've made up these things he supposedly said to you at your house to try to throw us off the track—to indicate that Malcolm was suspicious of someone other than you."

"No. No to everything you've said. I made no advances to Malcolm, and he made none to me. I'm not homosexual, and

134

I never had any reason to suppose Malcolm Ludlow was either. You tell me he was—personally I don't know. And if I were going to manufacture some quotes from him to throw suspicion on someone else, I'd sure as hell have made up something more specific!"

But Gene kept at him, trying to wear him down, asking him to repeat the same things he had said before—over and over. He tried to convince himself that they had grilled Chris Durham just as hard—or would when they got to him—and whoever else of the theater group they suspected . . . But he didn't believe they had. Or would.

Finally, late in the afternoon, they had dismissed him. They would want him back, he surmised, when they finished collecting their evidence.

He felt like one of Kafka's victims. None of this was real, and yet the threat was real enough. There was no evidence other than the fact that in the case of both deaths he was the last person known to have seen the deceased alive; but enough circumstantial bits and pieces could presumably be found and fitted together to make a case against him.

Yet for the moment . . . The fresh air had never smelled so good; the freedom of the outdoors never seemed so precious.

Now he was headed determinedly over to Alice's.

He only hoped that she would be home. He'd had no chance to call her to find out. If she wasn't there . . .

But she had to be.

She wasn't there.

He waited, pacing to and fro in the driveway and going a second time to the door to rap with the knocker, sending Poochie, within, into paroxysms of barking.

No use. And the futility and inactivity of waiting were more than he could take, so he got back on his bicycle and took off for home.

He had crossed the train tracks and was just coasting past the drugstore when someone hailed him. His cousin Leona, as he discovered with a backward glance. He braked to a stop and returned, taking his bike through the weeds at the side of the road.

"Ferguson. Hello."

"How are you, Leona?"

"I thought we'd see you at the funeral." He wasn't sure whether she was reproaching him or asking for an explanation.

"Oh. Well. I was unexpectedly detained elsewhere." He certainly wasn't going to tell her where.

She went on then to Malcolm's death, suicide as she termed it, bearing out what he had always thought about women: that they would rather talk about illnesses and deaths than anything else in the world.

She told him nothing about Malcolm that he didn't already know.

"I'm so glad to see that you're going around with Alice Jenner," she went on, "now that she's back in town. I've always thought she was such an . . . a girl with so much . . . spunk." From which observation (with the significant pauses in it) Fergie deduced that Leona had heard all about Alice's living with her boyfriend in New York and had not condoned it.

"Yes, Alice is great."

"You must bring her over sometime." In other words, Leona had put her mark of approval on the match—better that her cousin Ferguson take up with a girl of tarnished reputation (if not *too* tarnished) than none at all. That was another thing about women: like nature abhoring a vacuum, they abominated the sight of anyone going through life unpaired with someone of the opposite sex. Unless you'd taken orders in the Catholic Church, celibacy was the ultimate sin.

Glassy-eyed, he got away from her at last. He was always repelled by her lips, continually pursed as for a kiss. She couldn't help it, he guessed—it was the way her face was shaped, with cheeks so plump they pushed her lips out to the front.

And he felt guilty, thinking so unkindly of his only living relative. Only that wasn't true, was it? Her three children were also relatives. And equally to be avoided, if not more so.

As he passed the theater he saw that Chris's station wagon was parked by one of the exit doors. Chris was unloading stuff off the tailgate. What? Props already for *Blythe Spirit?*

No, that wasn't anything for the new production, he noted as he turned the corner onto Hill Road. Chris was carrying in a rolled-up sleeping bag and some bath towels and a portable radio.

It was today, he remembered, that Chris's wife was due back. Apparently he was moving in here.

Well, there was no ordinance against it as far as he knew. Unless Fire Chief Pennywith complained to the First Selectman and they dug up some old law dating from seventeen hundred something forbidding the domiciling of oneself in a public building. At least he'd give the guy credit for originality.

Chris, occupied with his goods and chattels, didn't see him, so Fergie went on by. He was delighted a few moments later to find Alice's yellow Vega parked in his drive.

No sign of her in it. She must be in the house.

She was emptying out the living room. Or at least that was

what it looked like—the place seemed almost bare. Much of the furniture, the fringed floorlamp, the Bohemian glass, and most of the bric-a-brac were gone.

"I thought Lotta Snead was going to take all that stuff," she said.

"She hasn't had time to come for it. What did you do with it all?"

"It's in the dining room." He saw that she had closed the sliding doors between the two rooms. Goodness! She'd shifted he didn't know how many pieces of furniture into there all by herself.

She had a dust cloth in her hand and was removing the telltale marks from where things had stood. "Doesn't this look better?"

"I wouldn't know the place."

"You don't mind, do you?"

"It wouldn't stop you if I did." He grinned. "No wonder I didn't find you home."

"That's where you were? I've been here for hours."

"I was at the police station for hours. Then your house."

"Oh." She stopped dusting, looking up at him with troubled eyes, and dropped into a chair. "Donna told me about Malcolm."

"The police seem to think I killed him."

He heard her quick intake of breath. "But I thought it was suicide!" She was sitting bolt upright in the chair.

"A case of slashed wrists usually is. But it may have been made to *look* like suicide. I think they're waiting for the autopsy results."

She was out of the chair; she was standing right in front of him, her hand on his wrist. "Why you? Why would they think you killed him?"

"Why would they think I killed Maryellen either?" He

138

could feel the lopsidedness of his attempt to smile. "The second crime to conceal the first, of course. Unless the second was a lover's quarrel, and the first was committed because Maryellen was trying to cut me out with Malcolm."

"A *lover's* quarrel!" She stared up at him, her lips parted.

"It seems that Malcolm was gay. I guess Gene Mack has really checked it out." His voice became unreliable; it shook. "I didn't even know it. Not a gesture or a high sign anytime, or if there was one it went right by me. But Gene Mack— and now Hyslop, too—just because Malcolm and I were friends . . ."

He was surprised to see a glitter of tears in her eyes. She put a hand on each of his shoulders and looked at him in a sort of measuring way. Her hands moved down his arms, sensuously, arousing him, until their fingers touched and she gripped his tight.

"You're the most gorgeous heterosexual guy I've ever seen," she said. "How dare they!" She leaned forward and kissed him.

Alarm bells went off in his head, and the feel of her lips blended with the memory of dreams and with the recollection of Sharon—but far surpassing that, because something new had been added. He felt a kind of tenderness he had never known before. He kissed her strenuously. He wanted to surround her, to possess her, to be one with her, and at the same time he wanted to protect her from everything— even from himself.

"Oh, Alice!" he said, hardly recognizing his own voice. They did it again.

"I love you, Gus. You can see that, can't you?"

"I don't know." He removed himself to arm's length. All he could think of just then was his bed upstairs, with Alice in it. It would take only a moment to undo the buttons on the stretch, tie-dyed shirt she was wearing, through which he could see the shape of her nipples, and then . . .

He turned away with almost a groan. "I don't know." He felt schizophrenic—half of him physical, half of him mental, and the two parts not able to agree at all on what he should do about Alice.

"What do you mean, you 'don't know'? I just told you! What you mean is that you don't know how *you* feel? About me?"

He faced her; the stag at bay. "I guess that's it. You're wonderful, Alice. I've always thought so. But love and marriage are for other people. I've never considered them for myself. I—"

"Consider them, then. Love, anyway. I told you I don't hold any brief for marriage." She reached out and touched him again, her hand on his wrist. "Oh, Gus, don't you care?"

He took her in his arms again and pressed his cheek to hers, stroked her hair. "Oh, I care!" And he thought of himself—an eccentric living alone, the world shut out of his life, a man whom the police suspected of being a deviate and a murderer. "But I can't be what you want."

She pulled back and looked up at him, and he saw that she was angry. "You're going to stay in your shell all your life? You're afraid to come out?"

"I'm not afraid. I don't know *how,* and it's too late to learn. I'm a solitary person. I'll never change." Yet he had changed already, since he had joined the theater group and since Alice had come into his life again. He was halfway out of his shell—and clinging in dread to the rigid security it offered? The known in preference to the unknown . . .

"You don't know what you can be like," she said, "until you try."

But it wasn't her words so much as her physical presence

140

that stirred something reckless in him. Now that they had embraced and kissed, he found that he couldn't bear it not to be touching her. He reached for her again.

An exhilaration like nothing he had ever known swept through him, like fire in his veins. He could do anything, *be* anything. There was no limit—

Oh, yes. There was a limit, a limit to how far he'd go with Alice, lovely Alice. He would protect her from himself and from her own intentions, which he could read in her eyes and feel in her every touch. He would keep her inviolate, whether she liked it or not.

They lay in rather improvised fashion on the narrow, hideous Victorian horsehair sofa, and he had taken her shirt off as he wanted to when he became abruptly aware of a third presence. A shaggy head was thrust between their faces; there was Monty, wagging his tail, eager to become part of this wonderful, friendly group.

Fergie swung his feet down to the floor, raised himself up, and pivoted Alice around so that she was sitting on his lap.

He kissed her once more, then moved her over, got up, and walked away. He patted Monty on the head and stood with his back to Alice, embarrassed for her to see his condition.

"You're going to stop because of a *dog?*" she asked him.

"Not because of the dog. Because I just wouldn't do it this way, Alice—take you on the living-room sofa on the spur of the moment. I think too much of you for that."

There was a short silence, and then she said, "Thank you. I'm glad to know it. I've thought you might believe, since I lived with Maury, that I was cheap and easy."

"No, you'd never be that." He turned his head to look at her and saw with relief that she'd put her shirt on and was buttoning it.

"About Maury. They told me that's where it was at, as

people phrased it awhile back. And after all the analysis I'd been through, I thought it was what I was ready for—that going to live with him would complete my therapy. I do believe in Women's Lib, too, and their tenets have sort of—" She stopped, looked at her hands, and clasped them together. "I'm making excuses, aren't I?"

"You don't have to, Alice. You're—"

"I think I do. On your account. You're enough older than I am to have quite different beliefs."

He strode quickly back and sat down beside her again. "Not that much older, and I'm not quite the mama's boy you may have thought. If you've assumed I was as my mother tried to make me be, God! I even fathered a child . . . though it was never born." He was gratified to see how startled Alice was—liberated, unshockable Alice, still more conformist and conservative at the roots than she supposed she was. And he felt a welcome relief to be confessing this at last to someone. "My mother paid for the abortion."

"When was this?"

"The summer before my accident."

She looked at him thoughtfully. "Oh, yes. Was it Sharon Kelsey?"

His brows contracted. "You know I can't tell you that."

"Donna Church's sister was in the same class as Sharon in high school." She stopped and he thought she had finished, but wondered why she was remarking on the fact. "So we all knew about Sharon. Cry 'pregnant!' and get paid off. She had more spending money than any other girl in Chillingworth. Word got around finally—no one would date her."

It was as though a window had been opened that he hadn't known was there. He could look out and the view was beautiful. "You mean she probably wasn't even pregnant?"

142

"Not very likely. She finally did get married, as you no doubt remember. You knew she supposedly had to?"

He shook his head. "I had nothing whatsoever to do with her after. I saw her wedding picture in the paper, that was all."

"She was reputedly pregnant at the time, but she never had the baby. Lost it, so I heard. Sometime after the ceremony."

"I'm glad you told me," he said, flexing his hands. "After all this time."

"I do remember your going with her that summer. I . . . I've always kept kind of an eye on you."

"Thanks," he said, smiling.

"So now where are we, Gus? You and I?"

He studied her—her short, tousled dark hair, her lovely cheekbones with the hollows under them, the softly curved mouth whose touch was so exciting. His eyes met hers that were like brown pansies—and he realized that he was no longer upset by her beauty. Had he been trying to put his physical side away all these years? Or had his problem simply been social unease?

Yes, where were they now, he and Alice?

"I'll have to get out of this mess I'm in. All this with the police."

"It'll get cleared up."

He smiled rather grimly. "I wish I had your confidence. Anyway, one thing at a time. And then I've got to get myself sorted out. After I'm cleared. *If* I'm cleared. I just don't know, Alice . . ."

She got up. "Okay. In the meantime we'll rearrange your furniture."

What she meant, he thought, was that she wouldn't pressure him on their personal level. But she'd be around.

And so would Gene Mack.

143

TWELVE

On Tuesday morning Alice found Officer Gene Mack on her doorstep. He had previously questioned her about the time at which she had last seen Chris Durham and Ferguson Brady after the opening night performance at the theater, but since that occasion her initial lack of enthusiasm for Officer Mack as a person (she'd thought him both sullen and condescending) had burgeoned into seething hatred—because of the way he'd been persecuting Gus.

"Come in," she said coldly, and they stood in the hall.

"I'd like to ask you a few questions if I may, Miss Jenner. About Malcolm Ludlow."

"I've never met him. I've only seen him on the stage—opening night of *Golden Boy.*"

"Oh. Well, what I wanted to know actually is about Ferguson Brady."

"Then say what you mean."

The corner of his mouth twitched in annoyance. "All right. What can you tell me then about Ferguson Brady's relationship with Malcolm Ludlow?"

"*Relationship?* That's a tricky word, Officer Mack, with

144

emotional connotations that do not fit the case. Gus and Malcolm were friends—barely more than acquaintances—and Gus was teaching him woodworking."

"But what was your reaction, Miss Jenner, to Ferguson's spending so much time with Ludlow—privately, just the two of them? When Malcolm Ludlow was a homosexual?"

"No reaction at all. I don't think anyone in Chillingworth knew he was gay, and that included Gus Brady. Maryellen Polk, after all, was a good piece of window dressing for Malcolm."

"Just because Ferguson denies having known—that's no proof he didn't know. Think back over the years you've been acquainted with Ferguson Brady. You could hardly say he took much interest in girls."

Alice drew herself up and narrowed her eyes. "And yet that's what the police first accused him of, wasn't it—being interested in very young girls—Sharon Kelsey, me, Maryellen Polk. It seems that Ferguson is damned if he does and damned if he doesn't. What you're conducting, Officer Mack, is not an investigation but a vendetta of some kind!"

He scowled, taken aback. "We've had two violent deaths now in Chillingworth, and in both cases Ferguson was the last person known to have seen the deceased alive."

"Ah!" she said. "So Malcolm *was* murdered—he wasn't a suicide. Otherwise it wouldn't matter who—"

"Look, I didn't say he was murdered."

"You didn't have to. And your point is that the last person known to have been with Malcolm is Gus Brady? Of course he is, because you've been too inept to uncover the person who must have killed Malcolm—and must have killed Mary-ellen, if the same person did murder them both. Tell me, have you accounted for everyone else in town besides Ferguson? Everyone who was at the opening night? Everyone who could have driven down the road Malcolm Ludlow lived on, at whatever time he was done in? . . ."

"But of the people who had worked closely with both—"

"People who'd worked closely with both of them in the theater group? That fits you, too, Officer Mack. In fact you were in charge of building the sets poor little Maryellen worked on. You saw her just about every day while the play was being readied. And where were you the night she was killed? Out cruising around in your little old police car. Did you cruise by the barn on your rounds just as she was coming out of there all by herself? And see your chance?"

He stood gaping at her.

"Do you have an alibi, Officer? For either of those nights?"

But when he had gone, no wiser than when he came, Alice wished that she had held her tongue. She had probably made things even tougher for Gus by antagonizing Gene Mack.

Indeed Officer Gene Mack was in a fury when he drove off. He felt pretty much as he had one time when he'd gotten his hand caught in the meat grinder.

Leona Wells phoned on that Tuesday morning and asked Fergie to have dinner with them. He must have been on her mind, he guessed, since their conversation the day before.

"That would be nice, Leona. When?"

"Oh, tonight."

Having dined the evening before with Alice at Cobb's Mill Inn, to which they'd repaired in her car after a struggle with the furniture, and there watched the ducks and the waterfall while they ate, he supposed he'd had his good luck for the week.

"Tonight? Sure, I'll come." He didn't tell her the acceptance was provisional; he expected momentarily to be arrested.

146

Yet the day passed without event. When by five o'clock Gene Mack and a deputy had not appeared at his workshoop door to take him into custody, he concluded that Mack and Hyslop were still compiling data, digging more deeply into his past, perhaps interviewing Sharon Kelsey, or whatever her married name was.

He went into the house and got cleaned up to go over to the Wellses'.

Frank and Leona were worried about him, it turned out. Because of the police investigation. The family was closing ranks and including him in, a gesture which he much appreciated in principle, though in practice it left him writhing in secret agony amidst the ruffles, satin pillows, and darling ceramic pussycats with gilt bangs and rhinestone eyes, while he listened to his cousin Leona's conversation.

Leona was one of those women who prefaced almost every sentence with "Don't you think that—," leaving the person on the other end of the dialogue in the position of either agreeing with all her inane pronouncements or being grievously rude and saying no, one did not think that—

She was like his mother, Fergie realized, in her belief that only one point of view existed: hers. His mother and Leona had by no means agreed in their views, and he wondered how they had managed to get on. By avoiding troublesome topics, no doubt.

"I really wanted to ask you, Ferguson," Frank said in a lull while Leona paused in order to draw breath, "whether you oughtn't to get yourself a good lawyer."

A sudden deathly silence fell.

They had not even discussed the police investigation, or Maryellen Polk's murder, or the fact that Malcolm's death had been intentional—on someone's part.

Fergie glanced from one to the other of them.

"You think it's that bad, then?"

Frank looked uncomfortable, stared down into the pineapple daiquiri that was Leona's specialty—Fergie had spoken up for Scotch instead. He took a sip of the frothy yellow liquid. "Well, it's the kind of questions Gene's been asking Leona and me. About you." He turned in appeal to his wife.

Leona dropped her gaze and smoothed the hem of her print dress over a plump knee. "Nasty questions, Ferguson. The kind of thing that only a person's own family would probably know about—anything that had been hushed up, that kind of stuff. Going way back to when you were a teenager—did you get into trouble then? Even did I think you were *normal?*" Her gaze flicked up to meet his, and he saw the genuine concern there and was touched. (Why hadn't he ever liked his cousin Leona? She was a nice person —a good person, really.)

Frank cleared his throat. "This homosexual angle came up, of course. Leona didn't want to say that, I guess, but you know by now, Ferguson, that since Gene found out what he did about Malcolm—"

"Naturally everything Frank or I said about you," Leona went on, "was all to the good—"

"Except that unfortunately I don't think we convinced Gene of anything. There's enough closet queens around and always have been, so that even if Leona and I had sworn on a stack of Bibles that you're straight as a die, he'd just have felt we mightn't know any better." Frank shook his head. "You don't have to prove anything to me, Ferguson, but unless Hyslop decides damn quick that Malcolm's suicide closes his murder case, your good name around town is going to be irremediably damaged by Gene Mack."

"You hadn't heard? There's a possibility that Malcolm may not have killed himself."

"*Not* have—? Oh, come on, Ferguson! Then they must *really* be playing cat and mouse games with you at the police station! Why, they had to break the door in to get to him!" Frank looked to Leona for corroboration. "Thelma told you that." She nodded. "So how can Malcolm not have killed himself?"

Ferguson shrugged. "You may be right. Maybe Hyslop's just trying to scare me to death, for practice. Maybe they won't know for sure how he died till the autopsy report comes back. But anyway, Frank, even if the verdict is suicide, that doesn't prove Mal was the one who killed Maryellen."

"I suppose not."

"And Frank's still right, Ferguson. You *do* need a lawyer."

"No. Not unless they formally charge me with murder. Getting a lawyer would only make me look guilty—as if I had something to conceal."

"But Ferguson—" Frank began, frowning worriedly.

"It's not as though I'm telling anything self-incriminating when I talk with the police. I don't have any guilty knowledge to give away."

"You don't know what you may be saying without realizing it. Even something innocent can come out looking wrong." Frank fingered the remnants of the scab that had formed on the long scratch on his cheek. Part of it had already peeled off.

"So they're not sure whether it was a suicide," he remarked thoughtfully a little later, when Leona had gone to the kitchen to get dinner out of the oven. But whether he had any speculations of his own on the subject Frank didn't say.

Ferguson did not know whether it was simply his gratitude to Leona for her concern over him, but whatever the cause,

149

he found during dinner that his dislike of Leona had evaporated. She was not his favorite personality in all the world, but he discovered that in spite of himself he was fond of her —and felt faintly sorry for her, though why that should be was not clear. Maybe it was because she tried so hard.

What she really had, he divined, was a galloping inferiority complex. And who could be surprised, considering the looks God had given her. What she wanted—wanted desperately —was approval. And she did not get it from Jenny, who was the only one of the children to join them at the dinner table. Jenny put her mother down at every opportunity.

"No, Mom, it's not like that at all. You don't understand—"

And a small death would take place in his cousin's eyes— the death of a bit of eagerness to please.

The reason she started so many sentences with "Don't you think that—" was apparently that she hoped to be right this time. The grammar should have clued him in long ago. She hadn't enough confidence in her own opinion to state it outright—she edged it in sideways, hoping for a blessing on it on its way.

Though if she was so lacking in confidence, how was it that around the house it always appeared that she ran Frank? Did he let her do it, out of kindness of heart? Or hadn't he ever discovered that her assertiveness was only bravado?

It was a short evening, as Frank was due at the theater. The Wellses had sandwiched him in between the workday and rehearsal of the new play because they had felt he needed them.

"I can drop you off at home," Frank suggested, as he rose from the table after consulting his watch. "We can stick your bike in the back of the station wagon."

"Fine."

150

"Or better yet, why don't you watch the rehearsal awhile?"

"Thanks, I've got some varnishing to do. But I'll come down soon and watch how it's going."

If I'm not arrested and in jail.

He said goodnight to Leona, thanking her for the home-cooked meal. Leona tended to cook meat until it was as hard and dry as a slab of oak, and she had apparently never heard of salt—but the pie had been good.

It was a mere five-minute drive to the theater. Fergie was repeatedly surprised these days, when riding in someone's car—usually Alice's—to find how close things were together by means of automobile as contrasted with the time it took him to traverse these distances on his two-wheeler. Even so, he preferred the bicycle, certainly. It got you closer to nature, you were exhilaratingly aware of speed as you never were in the confines of a car, and the wind in your face . . .

"I'll run you on up to your house, then."

"No need, thanks. I don't want to make you late for rehearsal."

"Well . . ."

So Frank parked his station wagon by the theater entrance, next to Chris Durham's.

"I hear Chris has found a place to stay," Frank remarked as they got out.

"He's camping here, I guess. At least—"

"Now, yes. But he's moving. Tomorrow, I think." Frank pulled open the tailgate door. "He's taking that apartment at Elma Seide's."

Fergie paused in the middle of maneuvering his bicycle out through the tailgate. "You mean the one Malcolm had?" he asked in surprise.

"Right. The one Malcolm had."

"Well, I guess it's available . . ." Something kind of callous, it seemed to him, about moving in where Malcolm had just died. "I wouldn't want it, myself . . ."

"No." But as Frank helped lift the bike down, he gave Fergie a rather odd glance.

Underneath all the family solidarity, did Frank suspect actually that his wife's cousin could be guilty?—that the reason Ferguson had said he wouldn't want to stay in the apartment was that he'd be reminded every day and every night of the boy he had slain in the shower stall?

"Well, goodnight, Frank." He put his leg over the bike and grinned, though the grin felt a little sick to him. "Thanks for everything."

He mounted and pedalled away toward home.

Even if by some fortuitous chance he was not arrested, would he ever be cleared of suspicion? . . . the suspicions even of those who knew him best . . .

THIRTEEN

On Wednesday morning Ferguson woke up with a wonderful feeling of having something to look forward to.

Alice had called him last night and invited him over. "Where have you been?" She had tried all day to reach him —when he'd been in the workshop and again when he'd been out to dinner. "I was hoping you could come to lunch tomorrow. My brother Hugh is here."

The eldest of her three brothers. He'd been several grades ahead of Fergie in school.

"Fine." And the family representative could look over the nut case Alice had picked for herself.

Was he going to ask Alice to marry him? he wondered throughout the morning. He couldn't, certainly, at this point —not with the threat of arrest hanging over him.

Was he suited, even, for life with another person?

The truth was that after thinking all day yesterday about Alice, as he had begun work on another of the chairs for his dining-room set, his feelings for her were still in a turmoil.

Well, with a third party present for lunch, no knotty decisions could come up—or overwhelming temptations.

It turned out, however, that he had not foreseen the day's real problem, which was that he could not bear to be with Alice now and not touch her. So he sat in misery six feet away from her while they drank white wine out on the terrace.

"I have a couple of days of meetings in New York," Hugh explained, "so it seemed a good chance to stop on my way down from Boston and have a visit with Alice."

"Luckily I have that daybed I got from you, Gus. He was able to sleep on it after a fashion."

With some difficulty, no doubt. Hugh was not tall, but the arms of the old spool bed allowed for a sleeper of no more than about five-foot-two.

"It's nice to see the place again." Hugh's dark eyes, which were like Alice's, rested on the silvered clapboards of the house in which he had grown up.

They talked about Hugh's wife and two children, and the home he had bought in Wellesley Hills, outside of Boston, and reminisced about people they'd all known in Chillingworth years ago—what had happened to this one or another . . .

Hugh was a solid-citizen type, putting on a little weight, losing a little of his hair, becoming somewhat smug along with his pleasant manner and a sense of humor that still functioned.

But who is perfect, after all? Fergie had always liked Hugh, and he enjoyed the conversation Alice left them to when she went inside to put lunch together.

At first, anyway. And then Hugh said, "Alice tells me you didn't care much for banking . . ."

"No. Not my line."

"And you've gone into furniture design now?" The question was put politely—perhaps too politely—as though he

154

had had to strain to put his query in acceptable terms at all. Hugh was a businessman, after all, and gluing legs onto chairs probably seemed to him not much above playing with Tinker Toys.

Fergie was glad when lunch was served—a seafood quiche, salad, and a beautiful square chocolate cake with fudge icing.

No talk of murder, thank goodness. Until just before Fergie left.

"I was wondering," Alice dropped into the conversation, "whether Officer Mack couldn't be our murderer—"

"Oh, Alice! That's not—"

"Why not? He was loose in his patrol car at the time she was killed!"

"But still—it's not possible!" Fergie argued, wishing that it were but not seeing a ghost of a chance of any such bonanza.

"Sorry you don't like the idea. Neither did he."

"Oh, God! You accused him?"

"Count on Little Alice," said Hugh.

"Oh, he couldn't have taken me seriously, do you think?"

"Well, I hope not." And to Ferguson, "Alice has filled me in, as you can imagine. Unbelieveable! In Chillingworth?" Hugh shook his head, and from the way his eyes skimmed quickly over their guest—as though the subject were one about which he must be sensitive—it would seem that Alice had told him pretty much everything.

Ferguson felt awkward when he shook hands with Hugh, who said he'd be driving on down to New York this afternoon for a dinner meeting.

"I'll call you, Alice." Fergie tried to convey to her more than he was saying—something that in any case he wouldn't have put into words. "And thanks for lunch."

She smiled with a special brilliance, and he got on his

155

bicycle and pedalled away, feeling a fool.

Alice was a free agent and would do what she liked. But it didn't help that he knew her brother looked upon him with contempt. Kindly contempt, maybe, but wasn't that almost worse?

The most galling thing of all was having to pedal up the driveway and out into the road with Hugh watching from beside his gleaming Mercedes. Ferguson Brady: anachronism.

Hell! The life he led was his own choice. And he'd have been better off to stick with it a hundred percent—not try to change himself into someone that would fit in with the rest of the world.

As he coasted down the hill from Alice's house, he thought back over everything she had said, every glance she had bestowed upon him. Did he mean anything to Alice really, other than a project she was working on?

It was only today when he was with her again that he had had this new, disturbing thought. It had been his mention of the homosexual business that had caused Alice, on Monday, to declare her love for him. Had the love scene he recalled with such emotion been merely an act of charity on her part? There had been that play, *Tea and Sympathy,* where a woman . . . If Alice thought he maybe did have homosexual tendencies, she'd be just the one to throw herself into his arms to prove to him he could make it with a girl.

Oh, no. No, no. That couldn't have been all it was—could it?

Fergie was right about Hugh's opinion of him.

"Why do you waste your time with a queer duck like that?" he asked as Ferguson disappeared from sight along the tree-lined road. But he saw from his sister's face that he'd

156

said the wrong thing.

"I happen to have a yen for him."

She left him and walked out the drive to the mailbox.

"He's no more queer than most people," she stated belligerently when she had come back with the weekly Chillingworth paper folded beneath her arm and several pieces of junk mail in her hand. "He's just more honest about being himself. People can be positively depraved, they can be anything behind a front of respectability and conformity, and who's to know? Like whoever killed Maryellen and no doubt killed Malcolm Ludlow as well. Our Chillingworth murderer is probably someone we see every day—one of the town pillars."

Hugh reached for the paper, took it from her, and unfolded it. "From what you've told me of the case, I'd be inclined to agree with the police. Ferguson Brady looks to me like a very credible candidate."

Alice stamped her foot. "Ow!" She had stamped it on a loose rock, and the pain in the ball of her foot was excruciating. "He is *not* the person who—" She broke off. "See? That's Malcolm there in the *Chronicle.*" She took off her shoe and massaged her injury.

"I've seen him somewhere." Hugh was frowning at the front-page photograph.

"You've seen Malcolm Ludlow? Not here—you haven't been back in Chillingworth since the family moved, have you? Six years?"

"That's right. But I've seen him. I remember the face because I was so struck at the time by his resemblance to Chad Currin. You remember Chad—local kid who was killed in an automobile accident a long time ago."

He lowered the paper. "I know now where I saw him. It was at the Berkshire Festival last summer—Tanglewood.

Jean and I drove over for one of the concerts. This boy was there, and he was with Burton Sayles."

"Burton Sayles!"

There was an amused smile on Hugh's face. He took her by the arm and propelled her toward the house. "No wonder Burton seemed unhappy that we stopped and talked to him. Because he *was* unhappy, believe me. I'm sure he hadn't expected to see anyone he knew, and he was embarrassed. He couldn't wait to get away from us."

Alice stopped on the walk. "Hugh, listen," she said earnestly. "I told you about the homosexual angle . . ."

"That's what I'm talking about! Burton Sayles would never in the world want anyone in his home town to know he'd gone up to the Berkshires for the weekend with someone who could conceivably be identified as a fairy!"

"Well, these days—"

"In *his* line of work?"

"Oh." She passed on into the house, with Hugh following after, and laid the mail on the old bachelor's chest in the hall. "I didn't tell you, Hugh, but the investigation of this girl's death did turn up Burton Sayles—sort of innocently on the sidelines. He was the one who was helping Frank Wells round up the horses in his yard during the period of time in which Maryellen Polk must have been killed."

"So? That makes Burton and Frank two people in town, anyway, who couldn't have been at the scene of the murder."

"Does it? I wonder if Frank Wells even looked at the time when he got home and found his lawn being trampled and eaten? Would you have? If—"

Hugh put a hand on her shoulder. "Now listen, don't start playing Nancy Drew! Keep out of the investigation, for goodness sake."

"Of course I'll keep out of the investigation. But when you

158

tell me Burton Sayles was linked with Malcolm, and undeniably Malcolm was closely involved with Maryellen . . . and now they're both dead.

"It would be interesting to find out whether Burton Sayles attended the play on opening night, and whether Frank actually knows what time he got home or just took Burton's word for it."

"Sis, let it be. Stay out of it. The police will solve the whole thing."

"Will they? And in the meantime Gus Brady is being hounded and persecuted and—"

"But you're not going to stick your little nose into the middle of things. Right?"

"You think I'm that stupid?" She tried looking her most dignified and mature.

"Possibly. And I'm glad you've got a dog, Alice—even if he doesn't do much! Keep your doors locked?"

"You sound as bad as Mom."

But when he had gone, setting her teeth on edge with his final words, "and find yourself a fellow with all his marbles," she stormed back into the house and dialed Gus's number.

No answer.

She put down the phone, thought carefully for a moment, and then went in search of the Chillingworth paper.

She found it where Hugh had left it, on a chair in the living room. Her glance rested for a moment on the picture of Malcolm Ludlow. If the homosexual angle was the key to both deaths, as Gene Mack seemed to think it was . . .

The ad for *Golden Boy* had the theater phone number. She went back to the kitchen again and dialed it.

"Chillingworth Little Theatre." A girl's voice.

"Do you happen to know if Ferguson Brady's anywhere around?"

"No, he's not. There's no one here but me."

"Chris Durham's not there either?"

"Sorry, no."

Damn! If she couldn't locate Gus, Chris would be next best, but . . . Maybe he had already moved to his new quarters. She tried the number she found in the phone book for Malcolm.

Not in service at this time. Well, not surprising.

She'd go over. The studio where Malcolm had lived—and died—was in the same general direction as Gus's house. If Chris wasn't at Mrs. Seide's studio apartment, she'd go on and maybe find Gus in his workshop.

Poochie, crestfallen, watched her go out the door, and as she backed around to pull out of the drive, she saw his paws on the windowsill of the empty dining room and the wistful face at the pane.

FOURTEEN

It was about three-twenty-five when Alice Jenner turned into the drive below Elma Seide's house and saw that Chris's station wagon stood on the strip of blacktop below the studio. She sighed in relief, parked behind the wagon's dusty rear window, and cut the engine.

It was about five after four when Ferguson, sitting in the fourth row of the empty theater studying the *Golden Boy* set while trying to visualize how the stage was going to look for *Blythe Spirit,* heard the main lobby door open and close behind him. He turned, expecting to see the tall, slouching form of the Chillingworth Theatre's director.

A slightly-built blonde girl was peering in from the lobby.

"I'm looking for Chris Durham," she said.

"So am I."

"Oh." She wandered irresolutely down the aisle. Not a young girl, as he'd thought seeing her from a distance and in a poor light, but a woman of about his own age, with an unhappy look about her. There were circles under her eyes, marring her delicate prettiness.

161

He got to his feet as she came nearer. "Anything I can do?"

"I'm Felicity Durham."

"Oh. Yes." Awkwardly he stuck out his hand. "I'm Gus Brady." He was mildly surprised that it was Alice's name for him that had come to his lips. He immediately felt more assurance, felt taller. Gus Brady was a name with guts.

"How do you do?" She was flipping a long envelope against the edge of her shoulder bag. "You're waiting for Chris?"

He consulted his watch. "He said he'd meet me at four to work on the set designs. He should have been here by now."

She looked at her own watch. "He must have broken his leg, then. He's never late."

"Probably ran into a snag in moving. The police have had the place sealed, I suppose—whatever that entails."

"Could be." She was studying the set. "How's the play?"

"Oh, fine. Chris's done a great job with it."

"He always does," she said, turning away from the stage with a little crooked smile.

She hesitated, then held out the envelope to him. "Could you give him this when he comes?"

"Sure." He took it and, without thinking, glanced at the printed return address. Seeing he had done that, she explained.

"It's about an interview for a job, I think. It may be important."

There had been a college seal next to the return address, which had been what—Bremmerton College?

He must have looked startled or blank, because her expression changed. "Oh. I see." She lowered her eyelids—over very large blue eyes—and then raised them. "You mean he hasn't told anyone that he was let go at Dumont . . . They

162

didn't renew his contract."

"No, he hasn't told anyone."

She looked up at him in sudden alarm. "Oh!" Her hand went to her throat.

"What's—"

"How stupid can I be!" She shook her head rapidly from side to side. Her hand shot out and she grasped him by the arm. "Look, can you just forget what I said? Naturally he wasn't going to let anyone know he'd been fired! He was going to wait till he had a new job and then say he'd switched posts voluntarily—lured away by more money or something.

"I'm so dumb!" She gritted her teeth. "I've been so wrapped up in my own problems I never gave a thought to . . . You see, with this murder investigation going on it would be a disaster if word got out about Chris losing his job! The police would immediately wonder why—what the trouble had been at the college, and—and they'd go up there and they'd find out."

With a shake of her head she pulled herself together and —he was sure it took quite an effort—looked confidently at him with a little smile. But her fingers, where they rested on the wooden back of the seat row, were trembling.

"It's nothing, really—nothing serious, I mean, except in connection with his teaching job. But I wouldn't want the police to get the wrong idea about Chris. He could have been in *no* way responsible for that girl's death—but it's how the police might look at it. He's a girl chaser. That's the reason Dumont College let him go. He—" She licked her lips. "He was always getting involved with his drama students—the pretty ones."

He could think of nothing to say.

"And that's what happened," she added harshly, "to our marriage."

"I'm sorry. You didn't have to tell me any of this."

"Well, once I'd let the cat out of the bag . . ." She sighed. "You must think I'm a mental case, telling you all this. I just about am. What with my mother's health problems and being cooped up with two small kids for week after week, I guess I'm ready to fall on the neck of the first contemporary I meet and blab my whole life story."

"Anyhow I don't think you need worry about the police zeroing in on Chris. They're concentrating their suspicions elsewhere."

"Oh." She frowned. "But just the same, you won't tell anyone about his losing his job?"

"Not a word."

"Anything you tell anyone in this town gets around."

"Consider me a dead end."

She laughed, seemed to relax a little. "You live in the big old house up the hill."

"Yes."

"I'm glad to have met you. I've heard of you, of course. It's just that we've never . . ."

"No, we've never." And of course she had heard of him. The town eccentric.

"I'll see that he gets the letter."

"Thanks."

But when she had gone he wondered where Chris could be. It was twenty after four.

And she'd said he was never late.

"Someone wants you on the phone." It was one of the pool of stage-struck girls who were always doing chores around the place. This one was minding the box office for the afternoon.

He strode up the aisle and out into the lobby. The girl—Susan, wasn't that her name?—a plump, anonymous-looking kid not likely, he thought, to be the next toast of Broadway, motioned him to the phone, which sat on a shelf against the wall behind the ticket counter.

It was not Chris on the phone explaining his absence. A girl. "Gus? This is Donna Church."

"Hi, Donna." He did not know Donna well, but was aware that locally she was Alice's best friend.

"Listen, something's wrong. Unless—you and Alice haven't had a violent quarrel, have you?"

"A quarrel, goodness no! I had lunch with her and her brother Hugh just a little while—"

"Well, listen. She called me here at the real estate office a few minutes ago and said she was leaving—to go back to New York."

"Back to New York?" he repeated stupidly, hollowly, visualizing Alice, beautiful Alice, setting down her suitcases at the door of the apartment she'd shared with Maury, taking out the key she must still have and using it, and flinging herself into the arms of this boor who—

"But she wouldn't do that," Donna was saying. "Not this way."

"What did she say, exactly?"

"That she'd gotten too nervous living alone here, and so she was moving back to New York. Just like that."

"Did she mention this character Maury?"

"No, and I didn't have a chance to. But she's *through* with him. Everything she's told me . . . Maybe I'm getting in the middle of something I should stay out of, Gus, but the fact is that Alice is a hundred percent hung up on you. Has been since both of us were in junior high. I know positively that she would not leave town as long as you're here. Not unless you'd kicked her down a flight of stairs and then trampled on her, I'd guess."

"Really?" He marvelled.

"Really. So I can't believe . . . Why don't you go over there, Gus, to Jenners', and just see—"

"Sure. If she's still there."

"Because it was so strange. She said she'd leave the key in an envelope in the mailbox, but not to bother showing the house for rent until she decides what to do with the furniture. What I don't get is why she didn't drop the key off here at the office on her way—she'd go right by here—And say good-bye, for instance? She's my best friend . . ."

"Yeh, that's peculiar, isn't it."

"I tried to ask her, 'Why so suddenly?' And she—well, she hung up on me."

"I'm on my way. I'll be in touch."

"And Gus . . . she didn't . . . *sound* right. Very stiff and stilted . . ."

"Okay, Donna."

But as he set the phone down he was thinking of the distance to Alice's house. It could be too late already—she could have left for New York; or if something was wrong over there—and what could that be? . . . He couldn't help thinking of Maryellen Polk lying raped and murdered in his woods.

He turned to the girl Susan. "Could I borrow your car? It may be a matter of life and death."

Her eyes widened. "Sure." With no question, no comment, she picked up a key ring from the counter and held it out.

"Thanks."

"It's standard shift."

"That's okay." He smiled and went out the door.

The car was an old Ford, a Falcon.

The years fell away as he slid behind the wheel. He might have been nineteen. One doesn't forget how to drive. A little rusty with the clutch was all.

He pulled out of the drive and onto the road.

Not only to Donna, but to him as well it seemed incredible that Alice would up and leave in such a manner. Alice was a very determined girl. After the sweat she'd put into fixing up the house and the trouble she'd taken over furnishing it . . .

And she'd said she loved him. Would she go without even telling him she'd change her mind?

A hundred percent hung up on you. She wouldn't leave town . . .

He pressed down harder on the accelerator, and as he rounded a curve the tires squealed loudly, to his rather grim satisfaction.

Even by automobile the trip took much too long, but at last he reached the weathered house with its turquoise shutters.

Her car was not there. The drive and the parking area at its rear were empty.

As he drew up beside the house, a cacophony of barking greeted him from under the forsythia at the corner. Poochie was here?

But if she had gone, she'd taken him. This must be a neighbor's dog.

He got out and crossed the drive to the former barn that had been made into the family garage, looked through the little window at the side but could see nothing. He unlatched one of the double doors, pulled it a little way back, and glanced inside. No car.

For the first time it occurred to him that Hugh might have

167

talked her into moving back to New York. But why would he do that? Alice's brother had seemed pleased to have her living once again at the old homestead. Nothing he'd said had indicated . . .

He tried the knob of the back door, but it didn't turn. He went around to the front and found it locked also. He banged the knocker, setting off the dog again.

The key would be in the mailbox, Donna had said.

It was.

He fumbled the envelope open and unlocked the front door—left it open and looked around. No one.

"Alice?"

How empty a house could be when you were looking for someone and they weren't there.

"Alice!" He took the stairs three at a time.

Her clothes, her things, were gone, although the bed was still made up, with the sheets and the quilted coverlet on it. A bunch of pansies in a yellow cream pitcher stood on the small, battered chest of drawers that she'd intended to refinish. But the drawers were empty, and there was nothing in the closet.

So she had gone . . . as she'd told Donna. Back to New York. To Maury?

Donna had been mistaken about Alice's feelings for the nut with the bicycle.

He stood there in the old square bedroom. Even with her personal belongings removed, the sense of her recent presence made the absence of her now unbearable. She had been in this place such a little while ago. This very place. Half an hour ago? Fifteen minutes? If only the clock could be turned back that little time . . .

How he had wasted these weeks while she was here! He could have taken her in his arms long since, made love to her,

168

taken her for his own to keep. Only this week—idiot! idiot!
—he'd told her he had to get himself sorted out! Oh, God,
what had been wrong with him?

Now he was sorted out.

And his whole world seemed as empty of life, as empty of
warmth as though he stood on the moon.

The one thing in the universe that he had ever wanted, it
seemed, was Alice.

It was as Ferguson reached the bottom of the stairs of the
Jenner house that he heard a scrabbling sound.

Quietly he stepped down into and across the hall and
surveyed the living room.

Nothing moved.

And then he heard another faint sound—a dog's claws
against bare floor.

He crossed to the fireplace, leaned down, and lifted the
brown chintz dust ruffle of one of the wing chairs.

There was Poochie.

Alarm coursed through him. Then there was the prickle
of fear and his mind cleared, confusion settling to the bottom
like dregs.

One thing was certain: Alice had not gone. Or at least she
had not gone willingly. Because she would never have returned to New York and left her dog alone here untended.

He hurried through the hall, as he did so closing the open
front door through which Poochie must have followed him
a few minutes ago from outside. He ran to the kitchen.

The police number was on a sticker on the base of the
phone, and in seconds he had Chief Hyslop on the line.

"This is Gus Brady. I want to report a kidnapping. Alice
Jenner—"

"Wait a minute! You're holding Alice?"

169

"No, you fool! I'm telling you someone has taken Alice and is going to kill her! He's already staged her disappearance—he had her call the office of Chillingworth Realty and say she was moving back to New York, and—"

"What makes you think she didn't go to New York?"

"Because I was here at her house for lunch just two hours ago and she didn't mention going *then!* Because Alice and I are engaged to be married"—She'd told him she loved him, and that was the same thing, wasn't it?—"and she would hardly move away without telling me! And because she's left her dog. She wouldn't do that."

"You're at her house? Any signs of a struggle there, forcible entry?"

"No. Her clothes are gone; her car is gone. It's a yellow Vega, Connecticut marker number JT 9311." She'd gotten the new license a few days ago, and he had put it on for her.

"Did she tell the real estate people why she was leaving so suddenly?"

"She *said* because she was nervous living alone—"

"Then that's why she's gone. She'll undoubtedly phone you from New York, and if you ask you'll probably find she's arranged for a neighbor to feed the dog."

"No! Alice isn't like that! She wouldn't panic and leave!"

"I'll send an officer over to investigate."

"Listen. You've had two murders in Chillingworth. Do you want another? I think the killer of Maryellen Polk and of Malcolm Ludlow is going to kill Alice and hide her body so that everyone will believe she went away."

"Describe Miss Jenner for me, please. And what's the street address? I'll send a car over there."

"But she's not here—she's someplace else. What I want is for you to put out an alarm for her! And I do *not* think she's en route to New York City. He's got her somewhere on one
170

of the back roads, some secluded place . . ."

"I understand what you're saying. Sit tight right where you are. I'm sending an officer to the house to look around."

But before the police car could get there he had gone. *Right where you are?* He could get arrested that way—Chief Hyslop could well be convinced that the town nut case had at last gone over the borders of sanity into rampant madness. But most compelling of all in getting him out of the house was his own mention of back roads, conjuring up a vision of miles and miles of secluded lanes with lovely stands of trees, leafy dells, ferny glens—all kinds of places where a body could be hidden.

"Come on, Poochie." He scooped up the dog from under one of the wicker chairs in the room off the kitchen.

"We're going to find Alice."

He drove like a madman, peering into every woodsy lane along the way.

Who was this person who had stood beside Alice making threats, giving orders while she packed, while she telephoned Donna? Threats with what—a knife? A cord to strangle her with?

The pale reflection in the windshield of Chris Durham's letter lying on top of the dash nagged at his consciousness. Durham! He'd taken such an interest in Alice from the beginning! . . . Chris Durham who was always getting involved with his drama students. The pretty ones, his wife had said . . . Gus could remember Chris standing with his arm around Maryellen Polk.

And where had Chris been, anyway, when they were supposed to meet at the theater at four o'clock?

At the next intersection he turned savagely to the left—White Birch Lane, another of the narrow blacktopped roads that twisted through the back country. It would take him in the right direction to get to Chris's—once Malcolm's—studio apartment.

"Poochie!" The dog was making a terrible nuisance of himself, crawling under Ferguson's legs and getting mixed up with the accelerator and the brake pedal.

"Here! Get out of there!" He pulled him out by the scruff of the neck and dropped him onto the floor behind.

That strange performance Mal had given . . . Of course! It was Chris who had understood that line of Mal's about being Hamlet—Chris and only Chris.

" 'The play's the thing'?" he had answered at once.

> *The play's the thing*
> *Wherein I'll catch the conscience of the King.*

Shakespeare's Hamlet, hoping to prove his uncle, the king, guilty of murder.

And what had Chris said? Something like "You know what happened to Hamlet—five acts and he's carried out dead in the last one. . . ." If *that* hadn't been a threat! Yet apparently no one had noticed.

Poochie had crawled his way to the front again and between Gus's feet.

But he had almost reached Mrs. Seide's. It was along here somewhere—past the red mailbox on the right. No, not yet . . . a little farther. Beyond the yellow house. Yes.

And Chris's station wagon was there.

No sign of Alice's Vega.

Leaving Poochie shut in the car, he ran up the steps and the walk to the studio door, thumped loudly on the panels, and opened it.

Chris lay doubled up on top of the rust-colored throw on

172

the bed. Gus first took note only of the fact that Alice didn't seem to be there; she was nowhere in the room.

"I'm looking for Alice," he said accusingly. Only then did it occur to him that the room's only occupant lay in a quite odd and unlikely position.

"You've come to view me on my bed of pain." The querulous voice was an old man's, its theatrical resonance gone. "Sorry I stood you up at the theater. I can't move—or hardly. I leaned over to shift a rug and put my back out. Slipped disk, I guess. It's done it before."

Gus was brought up short. He'd been so sure Chris had made off with Alice. He came over to the side of the bed and stared down at the bent shape, the pinched white face.

But Chris could look like that, too, if he'd just killed someone and stuffed the body into a makeshift grave. Couldn't he? Green about the gills?

"What have you done with Alice?"

There was a spasm of pain across the face below him. "I haven't done *any*thing with Alice. She won't let me. She was here before—"

"She was here? When?"

"About an hour ago. Is something wrong? You—"

Gus reached out and grasped him by the arm. "Tell me. Where is she now?"

"Ow. You're breaking my arm. She was going to the theater from here, to see you—I told her you'd be there. But she may have stopped off at the drugstore to talk to Frank." Chris was frowning now. Gus had let go of him and he struggled to rise, pushing himself up carefully and gradually, wincing with pain. When he was sitting on the bed's edge, he put his face in his hands. "God," he said. He peered between his fingers at Gus. "Listen, Alice has a hot new piece of information—maybe—concerning the murders."

173

"What is it?"

"She says Burton Sayles had a closet acquaintanceship with Malcolm. So she wants to know whether that alibi he gave Frank was on the level, or was he covering up for himself for when Maryellen was killed?"

"Oh!" Chris couldn't have made up this story—it was too far out to be anything but true. Burton Sayles? And Malcolm?

"Chris, Alice has disappeared. Someone's taken—"

"Disappeared!"

"Maybe that hot new information of hers was too hot. Because whoever killed Maryellen has Alice now—I'm sure of it. Burton Sayles? Where's your phone?"

"Disconnected. You'll have to try Mrs. Seide."

"No, you—I'm hunting for Alice. Can you make it over to the house?"

"I'll have to, won't I. Alice—my God! Here, help me up."

Fergie helped ease Chris to his feet, though his position was still the same as when he'd been sitting—he couldn't straighten up. Like a piece of bentwood, Gus thought, as Durham shuffled toward the door.

"She might have stopped to talk to Frank, you said?"

"Yes."

"Call Chief Hyslop and tell him that. And tell him about this Burton Sayles business."

"But how do you know that Alice has—"

His brief and disjointed explanation lasted only till they reached the Falcon at the bottom of the steps. "I've got to get going." He could see that Chris would make it to the house on the other side of the drive, and he let go of him.

"Oh, here." As he shoved Poochie over out of the driver's seat he grabbed up Chris's letter. "Your mail. Your wife

174

brought this." He handed it back over his shoulder and got in.

"But you don't drive!" The querulous tones floated in through the window.

"That was yesterday!"

.

FIFTEEN

A little earlier in the afternoon Frank Wells had pulled into his usual parking spot behind the pharmacy. He had gotten out of his station wagon and locked it.

As he was about to enter the pinkish-beige clapboard building through the rear door—he had his hand on the knob —Alice Jenner drew up beside him in her car and hopped out.

"Mr. Wells, I was just coming to see you."

"Hello, Alice." He'd known Alice almost all her life. She'd been a little tot holding her mother's hand when Frank's father had bought the old house that was to become the Chillingworth Pharmacy and the family had moved here. Over twenty years ago.

"What can I do for you?" he asked, thinking, as he had every time he'd seen her since she'd returned, how she had changed. She had interested him more, really, when she was younger.

She beckoned to him, and he stepped down again onto the asphalt paving.

"Gus had dinner with you last night, I know"—oh; it was

176

Ferguson she was talking about—"so I'm sure you're aware how pressured he's been by the police."

"Yes. Leona and I think he ought to get a lawyer."

"He won't hear of it.

"So he told me."

"Well, what I wanted to ask you about is this . . ." She was looking at him very earnestly, and he suddenly remembered that Alice herself had some kind of legal training. Why that should make him a little afraid of her he didn't know, but it did. He reached out a hand to the wooden railing of the back step and steadied himself.

"Mr. Wells, can you of your own knowledge corroborate the time at which Burton Sayles started helping you to round up horses the night Maryellen Polk was killed? Or did you take his word for what time it was?"

"Can I? . . ." He managed a smile of sorts, but his heart had skipped a beat and gone into a gallop. "What are you getting at? I'm afraid I don't—"

"Could Mr. Sayles have lied about the time? For his own reasons?"

"For his *own* reasons. Oh."

He frowned, shook his head. "I don't know what reasons they could be. *He* didn't kill Maryellen Polk. He wasn't even at the theater that night."

"How do you know he wasn't?"

"He said so, and besides I hadn't seen him there. But whether he was should be easy enough to prove—the ticket takers or the girls who seated people—"

"He needn't have been at the performance. He could have been at the theater, waiting outside."

He knit his brow, perplexed. "What makes you think Burton could have had anything to do with her death? I doubt that he even knew Maryellen."

177

"But he knew Malcolm Ludlow."

"He knew Malcolm? Knew him well, you mean?" Frank realized that his mouth must be hanging open, and he closed it. She was mistaken. She *had* to be mistaken.

"But I'd have known," he said, "if they were . . . were good friends. When I've worked with Malcolm practically every day, and when Burton lives right next door to me, I'd have known . . ."

"Not if they kept their relationship a secret. And there's only one reason, isn't there, that they would have. From the way you hesitated when you said 'good friends,' I'm sure you've suspected that Burton Sayles is gay."

"Exactly what are you getting at, Alice?"

"This. You know Officer Mack is hellbent to prove there was a homosexual affair back of both these deaths. And you know Malcolm Ludlow has been proved to be—"

Frank put a hand on her shoulder. He was no longer holding onto the stoop railing—enough adrenalin was rushing through his bloodstream by now to render him more than capable of whatever action or reaction was going to be required.

"Alice, I know you're very much concerned about Ferguson—as I am. He's a relative, after all, and Leona and I are extremely fond of him. But let's don't be in a rush to crucify someone else before we've got some evidence to go by. We'd better discuss this thoroughly, my dear."

He glanced around him. There was no one within sight. Customers of the pharmacy and of the grocery parked in front, not back here. "Let's see, where can we talk without being disturbed? Here, we can sit in your car, but let's pull over into the shade in the station lot."

She got into her car, and he slid into the passenger seat beside her. They crossed the train tracks, and Alice drew up

178

beneath the long, heavily leafed branches of a maple that overhung the parking area.

This was better. No one would see them here. There wasn't a train till evening, when the commuters would be coming home, and the view of the parking lot was screened from shoppers across the way by a high privet hedge on the other side of the tracks.

"How did you find out that Burton knew Malcolm Ludlow?"

"My brother Hugh was just here. He recognized the picture of Malcolm in today's paper. Hugh had seen him with Mr. Sayles at the Berkshire Festival last year."

"Well, anyone could be standing talking—"

"He says Burton Sayles was terribly upset that they'd been seen together."

"Or at least your brother thought so. Is Hugh still here?"

"No, he went on to New York. But he was quite positive about Mr. Sayles being all shook up—at running into hometown folks, it would seem, when he was with Malcolm."

"Well." Frank shrugged. "I don't know. You have some idea, I gather, that because Burton turns out to have known Malcolm he could be implicated in Maryellen's death?"

"Certainly he could. Maryellen might have been a continuing threat to his homosexual relationship with Malcolm."

"Hmm. What was Ferguson's reaction to this . . . this theory of yours?"

"I was on my way over to tell him when I saw you."

So she hadn't told anyone. Only Hugh Jenner knew of any connection between Burton and Malcolm, and Hugh had gone.

Frank was considering what to do. He said, "Burton has been at great pains, you realize, to keep anyone in town from

179

knowing of his . . . tendencies."

"But you knew."

"I guessed. But I don't *know,* you see. It's only conjecture. And he was married—"

"Which doesn't prove anything."

"No. But you mustn't barge in and ruin the man's reputation, destroy his name and his business in this town on the basis of some wild—"

"Exactly. That's why I wanted to speak to you first. If you're sure he couldn't have been at the theater that night at the time Maryellen was killed . . ."

His mind raced. The police must not learn that Burton and Malcolm were linked in any way. To stop Alice Jenner from telling them should he build an airtight alibi for Burton Sayles? Then perhaps she'd keep quiet.

God! The pressure Burton had been under and Frank hadn't foreseen it. How *could* he have known that Malcolm was Burton's secret lover? And yet, the fact explained how Malcolm had come into possession of the dangerous knowledge he'd had: Burton had talked.

"I'm thinking," he said. "Trying to think back . . ."

The vision of Burton Sayles being grilled by the police was one he could not shut out of his mind. There was no doubt about what would happen. If the choice was to come out of the closet or be indicted for murder, Burton would come out of the closet—and tell what he knew.

Nor was it sufficient for him simply to keep Alice from going to the police. She mustn't tell anyone—anyone at all —what she'd found out.

Alice must be stopped.

"The point actually," she was saying, "is not what time it was when you got home the night of the *Golden Boy* opening —it would have been five minutes or so after you'd left the theater, and at that point Maryellen was still alive, looking backstage for her sweater. It was right *after* that that she was killed."

"So what you want to know," Frank suggested, "is whether Burton was at home when I arrived."

"Was he?"

He must make this sound right. "I assumed—that is *later* I assumed—that he had been . . . because he said he was." He closed his eyes, trying to think clearly. "But was he?" His eyes opened again, and he looked thoughtfully at Alice. "Actually I was chasing one and then another of those horses for a good half hour or more before I gave up trying to catch them by myself and went next door to get Burton."

"Then how could he have 'pinpointed'—as I understand he did—for the police the time at which you had arrived home? If he wasn't outside with you till—"

He blinked. "He said my car lights hit his window as I turned into my drive."

" 'He said' . . . So you really don't know whether he was there."

"No. No, I don't. Maybe you're right. The police should be told about his acquaintanceship with Malcolm—and told he's a fairy, since they seem to be looking for one.

"Now, Alice, we'd better both go to the police. You can give them your theory and I'll tell them what I know."

She was pleased. "You don't mind shooting your own alibi all to hell?"

"I trust I won't be needing an alibi."

How could she have been so stupid, she wondered now. If only . . . if only . . .

"I'll just tell them in the pharmacy," he'd said, "where I'll be. Then we can go on over to the police station."

She'd driven back across the tracks, parked again by the drugstore's back stoop, and waited with the motor running while Frank went in.

He was gone only a couple of minutes. When he came out he stuck his head in the window. "I've got something here in my car that I believe I should show the police—after what you've told me. I'll be just a second."

She had watched him unlock his car and reach into the glove compartment for something. She didn't see what it was until he was beside her in the passenger seat, with the door closed.

Then she saw it. It was an automatic.

An instantaneous thrill of fear passed down her spine, as though she'd caught sight of a copperhead two feet away.

"We're going to your house, Alice," he told her.

Frank Wells? The colorless, harmless, kind-hearted man whose face she'd been seeing on the other side of the drugstore counter for as long as she could remember?

She blinked, backed up, and pulled the car around, ready to turn onto the road.

Gus's cousin's husband? In spite of whatever she'd said to Gus about favoring Frank as a suspect, she had never believed for a moment . . . Did Leona know, poor soul?

It had been almost an hour, now—well, more like forty minutes—since they'd left Chillingworth Center, and she had still gotten no chance to jump him or make a break to get away.

Surely Donna had known something was wrong; she might go over to the house out of curiosity. But it would tell her nothing, except that what Alice had said on the phone was true—she had gone.

Her things had been packed, ready to take to the car, when Mr. Wells had her make the call. The only problem had been

182

Poochie, who—bless his little coward's heart—had held them up for several minutes while Frank tried unsuccessfully to wheedle him into coming along.

"*You* get him," he had ordered her. But Poochie had not cooperated. He had hidden in the bushes and refused to come out.

"I'll come back for him," Frank Wells had said.

After he'd disposed of her, no doubt.

"You'll never catch him," she had predicted, turning in the direction he indicated as they came out of her drive. "He's terrified of strangers."

"I'll take care of him. Too bad, though—I like dogs."

What did he mean, "too bad"? He was going to come back and kill him? Poison him, perhaps? Because he couldn't be caught . . .

"You like people, too, I suppose."

"Some people. Not all."

He had sat as far over as possible in the passenger seat to minimize the chance of her grabbing for the automatic. He kept it carefully levelled on her and watched her every move.

They headed vaguely north—sort of northeast—in the opposite direction from New York City.

"Won't you be missed?" she asked him.

"No. I told them at the pharmacy that I was going off for a while with one of the theater group. Something about the new play."

"Donna didn't believe I was leaving town—just like that. She'll stir up a fuss."

"Not much of a fuss. It'll be evident that you did leave. Your clothes are gone, your car is gone, and you'll be gone."

"Where am I going?"

"You'll see."

"But when I don't turn up eventually . . ." He hadn't said

what was going to happen to her, but obviously she wouldn't be turning up, not anywhere.

"You will have disappeared in New York. Your car will be found there."

"And at that point my family and my friends will see to it that the police go over my departure from Chillingworth with a fine-toothed comb. What time did I leave? Who did I talk with? And Chris Durham will remember that when I left him this afternoon, all steamed up about Maryellen Polk's murder, I intended to stop off and ask you some questions about it."

He was studying her—a little taken aback, she thought. "You didn't see Chris. Not after you learned from your brother about Burton. You were coming directly from your house when you stopped to speak to me, not from the theater."

"Not from the theater. That's right. I talked with Chris at his new place at Mrs. Seide's."

"You're lying," Frank said coldly. "He told me himself at last night's rehearsal that he'd be at the theater all afternoon today, working on the new production."

"Well, he wasn't there. He injured his back when he stooped over to move a rug in Malcolm Ludlow's old apartment."

There was a short silence.

"I don't believe you," he said at last. "You're bluffing."

"You hope so. But you won't know positively till it's too late."

She believed she had guessed where they were heading. Chillingworth's own piece of wilderness, Witches' Glen. Kids drove out there sometimes to go swimming, smoke pot, drink, and make out. Or nature buffs came out to hike along the river, climb the rocks, look at the birds and wildflowers.

184

But there were never many people around—the area belonged to the water company and was posted "No Trespassing."

"My brother will wonder why I don't phone him tonight in New York. I'm supposed to."

Frank made no answer.

"And Gus Brady has a date with me."

"I imagine it'll be clear enough to Ferguson that you decided in favor of the other fellow, the one you've been living with in New York."

That hit home. It was exactly what Gus would think. Why else would she have left without calling him? And she should have known that gossip did trickle out to the old home town from the Big City.

It was then that she decided to wreck the car. It would *not* be found in New York. Gus was *not* to be made to think she had deserted him for someone else.

And let Frank Wells have a problem getting back to civilization without wheels!

But she should have done this earlier. Now there was no one about.

She waited until she saw a car approaching, so that there would be help of some kind. When she caught the glint of blue metal and chrome just rounding the curve ahead, she turned without hesitation toward the ditch on the opposite side of the road.

The Vega slewed across the pavement right in front of the other car. Alice had a glimpse of a yellow-haired woman in sun glasses behind the wheel of the gleaming Cadillac—her mouth hung open, but she had slammed on her brakes and missed Alice by a couple of yards.

Then they were in the ditch, the car bouncing crazily along, a boulder hitting something underneath. And

185

abruptly they were at a standstill.

The Cadillac had come almost to a stop. Looking back through the rear window, Alice watched it hesitate, saw a glimmer of the woman's pale face through the glass, and then the car accelerated and took off.

Damn!

Frank was glaring at her, still pointing the handgun at her chest.

"That was a crazy thing to do!" he said venomously.

"Maybe she'll report it to the police."

"Not likely. Her car wasn't damaged, and she could see no one was hurt—it was scarcely an accident. Now get this thing going."

"If I can."

"There's nothing wrong with it. We didn't hit anything."

He was right. Whatever had clunked against the bottom had apparently done no harm, and Alice was able to pull up onto the road.

"Don't do that again."

She would if she had a chance.

"I'll shoot—the second you start to pull something like that."

Yes, she thought, next time he would.

No reason it wouldn't still be there, Frank thought, the sinkhole up on a rocky, tree-covered slope. It had probably been scoured out by one of the underground springs that were so plentiful in this part of Connecticut, and the soil over it had fallen in. It had been quite a deep hole. They'd had a hell of a time getting Jeffrey out of it when they'd finally found him. Six years ago that must have been. Jeffrey'd been only three.

It ought to be more than large enough for Alice Jenner,

186

with room to pile rocks over the deepest part of the hole after he'd covered her up with leaves.

"A little farther," he directed her.

So that no one would see the car from the road, Alice thought collectedly, refusing absolutely to believe that she was going to her death. She had not survived a miserable adolescence, three years of analysis, a year and a half with Maury, and eleven years of fruitlessly loving Ferguson Brady to be killed just when happiness was in sight.

She drove slowly along the faint impression left in the grass by other cars, till the Vega had its nose buried in a clump of wild laurel and she could go no farther. The track into which they had turned from the road had already curved past a dense thicket and a stand of fir trees so that they must be quite invisible to any passerby.

This was better, Frank realized, than the old picnic spot he knew so well from the times he and Leona and the children had come here. They'd been unable to stop there, just below the dam at the reservoir, because the place had been taken already by a bunch of high school kids having a swimming party. As they had sped on by, he noted that the only parking place for Alice's car would have been out in the open.

Now the only problem was that he'd have to start from a different direction to hunt for the sinkhole. Shouldn't be too hard, though—he had only to follow the course of the little river back upstream. Nor were the kids they'd seen any danger to his plan—the sinkhole was quite a ways from the picnic ground.

"No, give me the keys," he said as Alice got out of the car, leaving them still in the ignition. (Hoping to get away from him somehow and drive off?) "Put them on top of the car." He pointed to the center of the roof, where he could pick them up without coming too close to her.

She reached into the car for the keys, straightened up, and with a vicious little grin flipped them away.

He did not even hear them fall. The crackle of twigs breaking under his foot as he lunged toward her, too late, covered any sound they might have made. Involuntarily he looked around: woods—tall trees and young, new growth—and underbrush everywhere. Windrows of fallen leaves from last year and other years before that. He'd never find her key ring in this wilderness! Or if he did, it could take hours.

"Damn you!"

"Born and bred in the briar patch, Br'er Fox," she chanted maddeningly.

"Get going, you little bitch," he snapped. "Along that path." He nodded at the trail, its start marked by a paint splotch placed high on a tree trunk. This would surely take them to the river.

She turned her back on him and walked ahead.

He followed carefully about eight feet behind her, near enough that she couldn't suddenly break away and escape him. He watched the motion of her buttocks in the dark green slacks, though not with any desire. Her figure was too mature. Not that she was fat, like Leona, but she had a woman's hips, and her breasts were much too fully developed for his taste. Womanly figures always reminded him of his mother, and that turned him off. Alice Jenner had been more appealing when she'd been about ten or eleven—soft and sweet-looking; round, childish face; her bosoms hardly more than two pimples swelling beneath the skin of her knitted tee shirt.

God, even Leona at one time had been a slim, pubescent little thing; that was why he had been so attracted to her. But long years ago now, her grotesque figure, its upper half propped up by means of something she called a long-line bra, its lower portion partially contained in a super-strength girdle, had become repulsive to him. It was only in the dark—dark dark dark—that he could bear to touch her, and then only because he was driven by his own needs.

After sex with Leona he always felt somehow defiled. On her account he was sorry about this uncontrollable revulsion —but not too sorry, because he was resentful as well. Why hadn't she stayed the way she was when he married her?

The path wound downwards, and soon they could hear the rushing of water. Alice hesitated.

"Keep going."

She turned, gave him a level look, and went on.

At the next bend of the path they could see the river below them, with a stretch of rapids. And it was then, with a tightening in his throat, that Frank realized they were on the wrong side of the stream. The picnic ground had been on the other side, just before the road crossed it by means of the concrete bridge. How could he not have realized he was on the wrong side? He had thought only of the fact that the road curved back there to parallel the course of the water and—

Well, they'd have to cross.

There would be no footbridge anywhere—this was not a recreation area, and anyone coming here was a trespasser. That there were trespassers in fair number was evident from the existence of the path they were on, but nothing would have been put here for their convenience.

They were going downhill and soon were travelling along beside the water. This whole preserve around the reservoir and along this part of the river was forest—pines and deciduous trees. Bushes, vines, creepers, ferns, moss, weeds, and wildflowers covered the ground everywhere except on the stone outcrops, of which there were many. Even those were

189

greened with moss and lichen, and in their cracks grew young saplings. This was all tumbled, broken terrain.

A sudden feeling of dislocation seemed to separate Frank's mind from the body that was walking, a gun in its hand, herding this girl Alice Jenner down the trail to the place where she would be killed. What was he doing here? How could he have been forced, finally, into this incredible situation?

The sense of unreality was fleeting. Oh, yes! He was here and what was happening was irreversible. All because he had at last caught up with Maryellen in Ferguson's woods and tried to quench the terrible craving he'd developed for her during the readying of *Golden Boy*. From the first time he'd come within three feet of her she had driven him nearly mad —so sexy, yet still undeveloped; with almost a child's body, yet behaving in that provocative manner. The soft skin, the honey-colored hair shot with reddish lights, the appealing short upper lip. It had been impossible to be near Maryellen and not think of intercourse.

When he'd caught sight of her that night just entering the back of the theater as he turned out the lights from the controls in the lobby, he hadn't been able to resist the idea of coming back for her.

Which was why, after half a lifetime of being careful, of going far afield when the urge was on him . . .

But the risk he'd taken in doing something like that so close to home had made him terribly nervous afterward. That was why he'd driven to Bridgeport the next day, when he'd had a chance to get away for a bit, and bought the gun, in case he should need it.

The walls of Witches' Glen loomed up before them now —towering rocky cliffs between which the stream flowed. Alice had to pick her way carefully from rock to rock at the

190

edge of the water, and Frank took warning from the way she slipped a couple of times on some wet surface. But she had leather soles and he was wearing Wallabees, which should keep him secure on his feet.

At least he'd learned from Alice how Malcolm had come by his suspicions. Because Malcolm had known something, that was for sure—that crack about playing Hamlet? And the look of loathing Frank had encountered on the boy's face during the performance had been unmistakable, something that wasn't in the script.

Now he knew it was Burton who had enlightened Malcolm. Burton had told him about the cooked-up alibi.

Surely careful, proper Burton would confide in no one else. Would he?

In spite of what Ferguson had said yesterday evening it appeared to Frank that the police—or the medical examiner or whoever—had not actually made up their minds as to whether Malcolm had killed himself. And if they hadn't? It would be so much simpler for Jim Hyslop, so much more satisfactory for the town administration, if Maryellen's death could be laid to Malcolm and the whole business written off as murder-suicide.

How could they tell about Malcolm, after all? Doc Clancy was no whiz as a medical detective. And the amount of alcohol Malcolm had consumed—surely that would fit in with the mental condition of someone bent on killing himself, drinking himself into a state of sodden despair?

Lucky all around that he'd drunk so much that night. Passed out, he'd been easy to deal with—the pillow over the face. Lucky, too, that he hadn't locked the door behind him when he'd come home earlier.

The thing had been so neatly executed. Surely the whole effort, with every detail seeming at the time providential, would not turn out to have been a waste?

If Alice simply disappeared in New York . . . Tomorrow he could drive her car in, and then he would take the train back. (Let's see—tonight he would leave it at the train station, where no one would notice it . . .)

And it was then, as he remembered her throwing away the keys, that he missed a step and turned his ankle.

Oh, Christ! Pain shot up through the bones from foot to leg, and he found himself suddenly sprawled in a stone declivity, the gun pointing across the river instead of at Alice.

She heard his fall and turned, but by the time she swivelled her head to look back, he had the Colt aimed at her again.

He smiled, partly a grimace of pain, and said, "Don't try anything."

"Of course not. Where would I go?" She gestured at the rocky walls on either side. They might as well have been in a long tunnel; there was nowhere here to take cover.

"I hope you hurt your ankle?" she said pleasantly, and Frank was annoyed to realize that she didn't seem to be afraid of him, not even with the gun held on her. Alice's manner was one of . . . one of contempt.

Well, she would not be contemptuous anymore when they came to the end of this little trek together.

"I'll be fine in a minute. You just stand right there and wait." He reached down with his left hand and felt his ankle. It was still very painful, but he didn't think it was sprained. He rubbed it and flexed it and it began to feel better.

He got to his feet and took a couple of limping steps. "Okay, go on. But not too fast."

Alice went back to picking her way along the rocky verge.

The walls of the glen were becoming lower. Soon, she knew, they would come out into open woods on either side. There was another canyon like this one farther on—though how far? She couldn't remember. But at the other end of the next long, high-walled glen one came out at the swimming hole. She'd been up and down the river here many a time with her brothers, Hugh, Bob, Howie. She thought of them with a sudden spasm of longing.

And Gus—dear Gus. But she mustn't think of him. She must concentrate on staying alive.

She looked back and saw Frank Wells scanning the water's edge ahead of them.

Good. He saw with relief that the path crossed the stream at a patch of shallow rapids and came out on the other side. There was a big splotch of white paint on the face of gray rock to insure that no one missed the way. And the path on the other side would be the one he remembered.

"Cross over," he called to her.

SIXTEEN

Burton Sayles came into police headquarters looking like a man condemned.

Chief Hyslop had had to ask him to come, instead of sending an officer over to question him at the funeral parlor, because there'd been no one to send. Every member of the Chillingworth force was out scouring the countryside for Alice Jenner.

He hoped this was all a false alarm, but after two deaths he couldn't take a chance. And especially after the second call, the one from Professor Durham . . .

"Sit down, won't you, Mr. Sayles."

He looked almost like one of those old-fashioned heroes from the days of silent movies—tall, meticulously groomed; handsome features, particularly the deepest brown eyes; dark hair with a bit of a wave in it; a sober and dignified manner, as befitted a funeral director.

Jim Hyslop cleared his throat somewhat awkwardly. "I understand that you knew Malcolm Ludlow. Knew him . . . perhaps rather well."

The "perhaps rather well," with all its connotations,

194

seemed to hang in the air between them.

There was a long sigh in the room. Sayles straightened in his chair and seemed to draw further on some private reserve of dignity. "Yes," he said.

"I almost came to tell you about it." Jim saw that the man was relieved, actually, to be here now and telling him. "Then Malcolm killed himself, and I was bitterly sorry I hadn't talked with you. It was too late by that time—there'd have been no point in it for me. Why lose *everything?*" His expression had darkened now.

"Mr. Ludlow's death was probably not a suicide. We believe he was murdered." The medical examiner's report was not in yet, but a good many things now pointed to homicide in this case.

The color drained from the handsome face. Burton Sayles swayed slightly in his chair."

"Murdered?" he said thickly. "Then I might as well have killed him myself. If I had come to you . . ." He stared into space, into a past now gone, its options nonexistent.

"Come to me and told me what?"

The eyes focused on Jim Hyslop. "Frank Wells. Frank forced me to back him up on an alibi for the night Maryellen Polk was killed."

"You weren't helping him round up horses?"

"Yes, I did that. But the time I gave Officer Mack was wrong. Frank came to my door later than I said he did. And it didn't take nearly as long as I said to get the horses back into the pasture. He must have brought them over himself, of course, through the gap in the fence."

"What time was it that you first saw Mr. Wells that night?"

"One o'clock or past. An hour later, at least, than I told Officer Mack."

"What made you lie for Wells?" Jim could guess, but he had to ask.

"He threatened to expose me—publicize the fact that I'm gay, though I don't believe that was the word he used. Before she left me my wife had talked to his wife, so Frank said. And then there had been an occasion several years ago when he came over into my yard, trespassing, into my fenced pool area. In *flagrante delicto*—isn't that the term? Anyhow, he knows enough to make my life miserable if he should choose to talk."

"You say he threatened you. Did he tell you why he needed an alibi?"

"Yes. He said one of the girls in the theater group had disappeared after the show and a search was being made for her. If there was 'any trouble' as he put it, he'd like me to swear I'd been with him from before midnight till around one, because he felt the girl was just the kind to get herself raped or molested. And he had this long scratch on his face, you see.

"He claimed he'd driven one of the cast home after the performance—a different girl—but that he couldn't tell anyone he had, because his wife is so jealous of the actresses he works with."

"Did you believe this story when he told it to you?"

"I tried to. And the next morning when I heard what had happened I tried to go on believing. After all, Frank could have come back past the theater and learned then that a search was on for the Polk girl—he needn't have been the one who had killed her. That's what I told myself, anyway. And he could have scratched his face on a branch. One is just never prepared to believe one's next-door neighbor has committed a murder."

196

"Excuse me." Jim got up and stepped into the department lobby.

Ever since Professor Durham's call they'd been trying to locate Frank Wells; Durham believed Alice Jenner had gone to the pharmacy to talk to Frank. Making Wells the last person to have seen her?

In the lobby Jim relayed into the microphone connected to the communications room the information, to be broadcast on the police band, that Frank Wells, for whom they were now urgently looking, was dangerous and might be armed.

Frank Wells. Almost a certainty, he thought. Because the search for Maryellen about which Wells had told Burton Sayles at a few minutes after one in the morning had not begun until after two-fifteen, when Mr. Polk had phoned the police.

Jim Hyslop sat down again at his desk. "Did you tell Ludlow of this conversation with Frank Wells?"

"Yes. On the following night—Friday night. When I got home after seeing the play Mal was waiting for me, and we talked. He was worried—worried sick—that the police would believe he'd killed the Polk girl."

Sayles leaned forward as though about to plead for something, his hands clasped so hard together Jim wondered if he wouldn't fracture a finger. "The thing that's been so terrible for me, Chief Hyslop, is that *I* was Malcolm's alibi. But I wouldn't let him give you my name. After a lifetime of caution, I couldn't risk . . . and I'd already lied to the police; I didn't want to retract what I'd said to Officer Mack. I was sure Mal would be cleared without my getting involved."

"He was with you the night Miss Polk was killed? After the performance at the theater?"

"Yes. He stopped by to tell me how it had gone. He was there, in fact, when Frank came to the door about the horse business, which Frank couldn't have guessed, because Malcolm had put his car in my garage—a precaution we always took."

"But you said it wasn't till Friday night that you and Ludlow discussed the alibi Frank Wells asked you to—"

"That's right. When I came in from helping Frank, Malcolm had gone. He must have backed out quietly, with his lights off. I suppose Frank and I were by the stone fence behind his house, because I didn't know Malcolm had gone till I came in and found the note he'd left."

"Frank Wells knew that you and Malcolm Ludlow were friends?"

"I wouldn't have supposed so. I've made sure my private life was very private indeed. No one in town has known I was even acquainted with Malcolm."

"Have you any personal knowledge of Ludlow's death?"

A quick grimace of pain passed over Sayles's features. "No. But you tell me now it was murder. I think it must have been Frank Wells, then, who killed him."

"That's only a guess?"

"Only a guess. But after our conversation Friday night Malcolm was convinced Frank was guilty of killing the girl. Thinking back now on what's happened, I realize that as volatile a person as Malcolm was, he could never have gone on stage Saturday afternoon with Frank and not given some very plain indication of what he felt. Frank must have decided he would have to shut him up before he actually talked."

"Did you speak with Ludlow after that performance?"

"No. I was out that evening. I tried to phone him Sunday, but of course he didn't answer."

198

An uncontrollable shudder passed over Burton Sayles's long frame. He was remembering again how he had received the news that Malcolm was dead. At the end of the services for the Polk girl Officer Tully had unexpectedly come up to him and had told him, never imagining, certainly, that this death meant any more to Burton than a headline in the paper and perhaps a piece of business for him.

He'd thought he couldn't bear it—not only Malcolm's dying like that, so suddenly, so unpredictably, but he'd felt the suicide was his fault. Now it seemed that Malcolm hadn't, after all, killed himself—yet the guilt was no less.

"If I had come to you with the truth, Chief Hyslop, Malcolm would be alive . . ."

He stopped and sighed. "If it's possible to treat all this in confidence . . ."

"I'll do what I can. Depends on how things develop."

"I'd appreciate it. My grandfather built up our mortuary business, and my father after him. It's a . . . a calling, you know—in some ways like belonging to the ministry." The dark eyes rested somberly on Jim's. Yes, the man would have made a capable preacher. "If this were New York City, for instance, or San Francisco or Los Angeles. But Chillingworth? There's still a lot of bedrock New England about this town in spite of the new people, the commuters. A funeral home here—you understand my position, I'm sure, Chief Hyslop. With people's loved ones passing through my hands . . ."

A new street had been bulldozed into the woods off Hermit Lane, with half a dozen lots cleared and two houses started. At this hour the workmen had been gone for some time. Gus turned into the rutted dirt roadway, visualizing Alice buried where tomorrow or the next day concrete would be poured, sealing her secretly away forever beneath someone's basement floor.

He left the motor running, thought of using Poochie as a bloodhound but feared he'd lose him, so left him shut in the car.

The raw earth was packed hard and unevenly—footmarked, littered with builders' trash. Both basements were in and covered by the grid of two-by-tens that would support the flooring over them. He peered in—neat and empty. He clambered over piles of dirt and leaped trenches, examining every place that could be a natural grave.

She wasn't here.

He thought next of the town dump and drove out Old Danbury Road to the fenced-off acreage of junk and refuse.

Aware of the grotesqueness of coming here to look for vibrant, lovely Alice, he pulled up to the padlocked gate. This was all insane, insane. He must be mistaken about the whole thing. Alice had left him for the guy in New York—

The sign on the fence gave closing time as 4:00 P.M. A rush of relief—the place had probably been locked for the night before whoever it was could have brought Alice here. And Gus's momentary doubt had gone again—the doubt of his sanity, of Alice's peril. Burton Sayles had taken Alice. Or Frank—yes, it could be Frank who had taken her away.

And where else could he—

Witches' Glen.

Why not Witches' Glen? A wilder, more—

He leaped into the Falcon again and was off. He was part way there already, here at this end of Old Danbury Road.

If Frank Wells had taken Alice—and it seemed fairly certain that she must have stopped at the pharmacy to talk to him, on her way from Chris's to the theater . . . Ferguson was thinking of the many times Frank must have been to

Witches' Glen—with the Bradys, with Leona. The Ferguson family had picnicked there for a hundred years or more— since before the Hydraulic Company had owned it or ever thought of building the dam.

Frank. And Maryellen?

A sudden recollection of Leona coming into the kitchen at home, a Leona in shock. Eight or ten years ago . . .

She had rushed over from her house to tell Gladys about the girl who'd been found—nude, strangled, stuffed under a pile of brush in the woods. The younger sister of an old friend of Leona's who'd lived in . . . Milford, was it? No, Hamden. A girl of about thirteen.

"And so pretty," Leona had told his mother. "We'd just seen them all—Frank and I had—a couple of weeks ago, for the first time in years."

Hamden. A forty-mile drive from Chillingworth.

He sped around the curves, his hands clamped on the wheel.

Around the next curve and he would be able to see the reservoir.

No. Wrong curve.

But soon.

He passed a small yellow sign on a tree. And another.

PUBLIC WATER SUPPLY
NO TRESPASSING
HUNTING OR FISHING

He scanned the road ahead for any indication of a car having pulled off at the side, although Alice's Vega could be long gone, and she could have been left dead anywhere by a man who was driving her car miles away by now.

At last Chillingworth Reservoir lay ahead of him, a long

201

stretch of water lying darkening in the late afternoon light.

He slowed as he neared the dam, on the left side of the road, where the water poured over to form the river. The water foamed and raced under the bridge, only to quiet down on the other side, spreading out into a large swimming hole.

Just short of the concrete parapet of the bridge two cars were parked below the road, on the right, by the pool.

He slammed to a stop.

Neither car was Alice's.

A boy of sixteen or seventeen in dripping jeans stood on the great rock he and Chad and Don had always used to dive from.

"Hey!" He yelled out the window and got out. No one could hear him at any distance because of the roar of the water going over the dam.

The kid, hands on his hips, watched as Gus made his way down the slope from the road and leaped to a rock just above him.

"Have you seen a girl and a man anywhere here in the past hour?"

The boy shook his head. "Nobody but us."

"Then did a yellow Vega go by here?"

The kid shrugged. "I wouldn't know." He dove in—as a kid named Fergie had, too, in his time, from the same spot —being careful not to break his neck, because the water wasn't deep enough here to dive in safety.

There were three others on the far side of the pool, two girls and another boy, laughing and bobbing up and down in the water. Even if he could attract their attention they couldn't hear him. Nor would they, he imagined, have been much aware of traffic going by—except for the police, since it was illegal to swim here.

He climbed back up the bank and got in the car that

belonged to Susan. He had just put it in gear when he heard a shrill whistle above the water's roar.

The boy he had talked to was signalling him.

He got out again and so, inadvertently, did Poochie. Ferguson leaned over the guard rail at the edge of the road, and the boy climbed up a little way from the water.

"There *was* a yellow Vega!" he shouted.

One of the girls, waist-deep in the pool, was waving and nodding. She pointed up the road in the direction in which he was headed.

"Twenty minutes—maybe half hour ago." The information was relayed from girl to boy to Ferguson. The boy, too, pointed to the road which curved away from the reservoir. "Went that way."

"Thanks!" He waved to the group in acknowledgment. A half hour? And where were they now? He looked around for the dog. Under the car. He pulled him out, aware of time rushing by, life running out.

They had come to the end of the first glen, to the open woods. Here the path divided, one branch continuing at water's edge, the other going uphill.

It was the uphill one he wanted.

"That way," he directed her, trying to remember how far he and Leona had had to come—from the other direction, upstream—hunting and calling, after Jenny had come running back along the path to tell them she'd lost Jeffrey.

His eyes searched the hillsides above them—what he could see of them through the stands of trees. He thought the sinkhole was on the side of this next hill, the one through which the river had cut another glen. It should be about two-thirds of the way up.

He saw nothing like the spot he remembered. Hell. Damn.

"You know we're fairly close by now to where those kids are," she said, "the ones who were swimming. If you fire at me they'll hear."

"No." Frank had a comforting mental image of the water pouring over the dam above the bridge, where the reservoir overflowed into the stream. "They'd never hear a shot over the sound of the waterfall.

"And they're still too far away," he added, "to do you any good."

He was right, of course. The hope that he might be reluctant to fire when she made a break was quickly extinguished. She was going to be very much at risk.

She had noticed that he was looking for something, searching the terrain around them.

She, too, studied the rugged hillside above—its surface of rock outcrops interspersed with clumps of trees, the tangle of vines and undergrowth that covered the ground between the rocks, and the decaying trunks of trees felled in the last ice storm or uprooted by a high wind. And she felt at last, as she had not before, the mortal danger in which she walked.

They had arrived, she sensed, at the location he had in mind. Places in which to hide a body were everywhere.

Not a bird flew over them or twittered in a tree; not a squirrel, not even a snake was on hand with two watching eyes to witness what might happen here.

She had a feeling her only chance was now.

She watched; she waited for an opportunity—any opportunity.

It must be soon.

A long, skinny tree branch hung across the path at chest height. It was the first chance to present itself to Alice—and perhaps the last to be offered her.

204

She stopped just short of the branch and, raising one foot, pretended with her forefinger to search out a pebble from the inside of her shoe. It was sufficient pause to bring Frank a little closer behind her. When she went on, she was holding the branch, and she held onto it as long as possible, bending it into a natural weapon.

She let go and the branch whipped back.

Alice took off up the path. Behind her she heard an exclamation as the young, limber switch connected with its target. The impact would spoil his aim at the very least, and the clusters of leaves might cut off his view of her—momentarily.

She tore on up the path, which was steep here, her feet slipping now and again on rocks. A turn to the right, and she bent low, because the bushes to either side here were not tall enough to hide her.

He fired. She heard the bullet hit the hillside ahead of her.

She climbed faster, and he fired again.

Missed.

There was dense foliage along this part of the trail—trees on either side, and sheltering vines. She could hear him coming behind her. He had stopped before to take aim, she thought, which had given her a little leeway, but now he was catching up.

At the next turn of the path her stomach sank in cold fear. The way lay up a rock cliff. She could climb it only by using hand holds and levering herself up slowly and laboriously for a distance of at least twenty or thirty feet. Frank Wells with his automatic would be able to pick her off at will, long before she could reach the top.

She left the trail and cut off to the side, toward a giant boulder. Hurriedly she slipped behind it and surveyed the lay of the land. The ground dropped abruptly away to the river here.

And escape down the long, nearly vertical descent would be out of the question. The way was too exposed; there was nowhere she could hide from a man shooting at her from above. That he would hear her going down was certain, as well. Small stones and little patches of gravel that had been washed from higher up lay everywhere along the crevices of the rock face, impossible not to dislodge in the course of her flight.

A hundred feet below, perhaps, the river glimmered cooly, brown and clear, its waters unmuddied here where it ran over rock. It was the same river that flowed behind the house where she had grown up and was living now—the old Jenner house, no more than five or six miles away. And it might as well be across the continent.

She was trapped, helplessly trapped.

"I saw you," he said from quite near. "I saw where you went. Come out of there!"

Alice nestled into a hollow at the base of her boulder.

He checked the track on into the woods—not with any particular hope. That had gone now. Too much time had elapsed. But in case they had been here and had left some trace . . .

And there it was: Alice's car.

He scrambled out, tripping over the dog. He listened.

Nothing to hear. He looked into the car. She wasn't there. The back seat was packed to the window level with her personal things.

No bloodstains . . .

Where the old tire impressions faded out there was the start of a path. He bent low and inspected it, and found nothing to indicate that anyone had passed this way. But Poochie, after nosing in small circles around the car, discovered clues of his own and went tearing off, muzzle close to the ground.

Ferguson followed at a run.

As he leaped a low, muddy spot he checked and came back. Yes, two different-sized shoes had made prints in the moist earth of the path.

He sprinted on, though all alone now. The dog had disappeared.

Would Poochie give tongue when he got close? Oh, heavens, no. Only bloodhounds tracked human beings. Poochie's ancestors, whatever they were, would have been trained on small animals.

He slowed at last in order to listen—and heard nothing but the gurgle of the river.

He was halfway through the first of the two rocky chasms that comprised Witches' Glen. He stared toward the far end. Where was she?

He continued on, leaping from rock to rock along the edge of the water, where there was now no path, only a jumbled stretch of fallen stone. He eyed the water, shallow through here. Had it been deeper where river and path first met back there? Deep enough to drown someone and sink the—

He had almost reached the end of the canyon when he heard the shot.

He froze for a moment, and there was a second shot. The sound had come from up ahead.

Ferguson plunged on, wading the river where the trail crossed.

Although Gene Mack had taken a distinct dislike to Alice Jenner, she had suddenly become of prime importance to him.

Finding Alice, and finding her alive, was something he felt

he owed to Ferguson Brady. Amends, sort of, for the hard time he had put the guy through. He'd never *apologize*, certainly—it wasn't necessary for a police officer to apologize to anyone he had grilled in the line of duty, even if the suspect turned out to be pure as the driven snow. But still, Gene knew he had been nasty to Ferguson over and beyond what was called for.

A personal thing. And why? Well, because Ferguson lived in that big old house up on the hill and felt he was too good to work—and got away with it because he'd been born into one of the town's First Families.

Somewhere at the back of Gene's mind floated the recollection of another family who had lived in a big old house on a hill, a family for whom his father, all during Gene's boyhood, had worked as a chauffeur, branding his child forever as the son of the help. Yet Gene did not consciously make the connection. He seldom thought of his father anymore—he'd been dead for years.

Gene had been in Chief Hyslop's office when his boss had received the call from Ferguson, and it was then he'd found out that Alice Jenner was actually Ferguson's fiancée—not that either he or the Chief had taken that call very seriously at the time. But now, after the further information from Chris and then the facts Hyslop had gotten from the funeral director, whatever they were . . .

Frank Wells. Who would ever have believed it? The Chief, at least, seemed to be convinced it was Frank they were after.

Frank's car was parked at the pharmacy but he wasn't there.

When Gene reached the pool below the dam at the beginning of Witches' Glen, he found it full of kids. One look at his flashing roof lights and they were scrambling out of the

208

water, grabbing for their things, assuming he'd arrived to bust them.

He pulled off at the side of the road and ran down the slope beside the bridge.

"Seen anything going on around here?" he asked the nearest boy, who was looking at him defiantly while buttoning his shirt.

The kid shook his head. "Some man was looking for a yellow Vega is all. It went thataway"—he pointed—"and so did the guy."

The information about the car jibed with the report on where it was now. But the guy? Frank? "Well, you kids clear off. You know you're not allowed here—it's posted." He turned away and headed for the well-defined path that led into the trees.

They were here, all right—Frank and the girl. Neither of them could have come out this way onto the road without the swimmers seeing them. John Tully had found Alice Jenner's car, with her stuff in it, parked a mile and a half beyond here, just off Glen Road. Tully was going in from that point, and Gene was to take the path from this end, working toward his fellow officer.

He was glad he'd been so near the reservoir when the call had come in on his radio. This case had been his to begin with, and he wanted to be in on the finish of it.

As he entered the woods, Gene unsnapped the flap of his holster.

She was sure by now that he'd been bluffing. He had not seen where she had gone. He was crashing around in the bushes looking for her, but in the wrong direction.

Yet he would know she was near. It was only a matter of

time before he would have searched all the surrounding ground and would know where she must be.

She looked down again. No way. No way to descend without his hearing her and then seeing her.

"You're behind the big rock," Frank said suddenly with the smugness of certainty. He sounded as if he were about twenty feet away.

She faced the boulder, hands touching its side. It was a mottled brown and white with little striations of green, and the feel of it under her fingers was reassuring. It was a foot or so higher than her head, and over its top she could see the steep rock face she had been unable to climb to possible safety. A long step back was the drop-off toward the river below. But there was room enough for her to play ring-around-the-rosy with the bulk of the rock between her and Frank Wells—for a time, at least.

He would come from her right, she thought, from the direction of the rock cliff in front of her.

What was he doing? Was he moving toward her now? Again she became aware of how silent these woods were. Not even the mosquitoes that hovered and danced around her, ready to light, made any sound.

Incredibly, she heard him from behind her, to the left. With a quick intake of breath she turned her head toward where he must be. He had gone down the path again, then, and was sneaking up from that direction to surprise her?

Carefully she stepped to her right. One step—quiet, making no noise. Another step. Careful. She looked back over her shoulder and could see nothing, but she heard the rustle of leaves and a soft footfall.

She took another step around the rock, in away from the drop-off, putting solid stone squarely between herself and the

210

stealthy climber. And came face to face with Frank Wells, who was not behind her on the other side of six feet of rock at all, but was standing at the bottom of the rock wall ahead, nearly close enough to reach out and touch her.

Sweat glistened on his face, and he was in a state of considerable dishevelment. But when he saw her he smiled, anxiety giving way to jubilant relief.

Gene came out on top of the escarpment—and could hardly believe his luck.

There was Alice Jenner, no more than twenty-five feet below him, hanging onto a big rock near the edge of the bluff.

He did not call out to her, because he wanted first to locate Frank. He was here, Gene knew from the girl's stance. She was hiding from him, trying to ease away.

And then as his eyes searched the brush and trees below him they caught a movement beyond Alice Jenner. A man was creeping stealthily up toward her over a rock outcrop.

Good God! It was Ferguson Brady! Gene's mind flashed back to his conversation with Chief Hyslop. What had he said exactly? Whatever Burton Sayles had told the Chief had not been relayed, so Gene didn't know what it was. The Chief had said the man they were after was "Frank Wells, almost without a doubt." Well, here was the doubt, and the Chief was mistaken. Gene had only to watch the girl's fearful retreat from her pursuer and see the grim, purposeful expression on the face of Ferguson Brady as he climbed up toward her to know that here was his killer.

Gene had been right about him and about the case all along.

"Stop or I'll shoot!" he called.

Ferguson did not stop—he moved faster. Gene Mack took

a step forward, aimed his .357 magnum carefully at the man he had so disliked from the moment they had met, and fired.

Gus had not called out to Alice when he finally spotted her, for fear of startling her. From where he stood she appeared to be poised on the very edge of a cliff. One wrong movement and she could plunge into the gorge.

He did not yet know where her captor was, his adversary. (Was it Frank?) That was another reason he did not call out. He must locate him before giving away his own presence here.

He climbed silently up the path. Ah, he could hear someone moving around on the other side of a clump of saplings. Someone hunting Alice? Or was he preparing some sort of grave for her, knowing exactly where she was and that he had only to collect her and put her in it?

Now the man he could not see had moved farther away, moved toward the place he knew Alice to be.

Gus was closer to Alice than to the other person, who had reached a point quite a bit above him on the trail—he could tell from the sound of the man's progress over a gravelly surface above him. He must try to be the first to get to Alice.

He left the path and climbed fast over a rock outcrop. Glancing up, he saw that Alice was no longer where she had been. Now she was on the far side of the huge boulder to which she'd been clinging. Only her fingers were still visible to him as she edged around it, going away from him.

"Stop or I'll shoot!"

An echo from the far side of the glen wall distorted the words as the last one reached him, so that he could not recognize the voice. He had no time even to wonder whose it was, though he was aware of faint surprise at the direction from which it seemed to come. Direction and sound both were warped, he thought, by the shape of the glen.

He could only leap madly after Alice now, for she had disappeared beyond the rock.

A bullet whined overhead and the sound of the shot echoed and re-echoed through Witches' Glen as his feet slipped on worn and weathered stone and he stumbled over a crevice.

Above him, unseen by any of the party below, Gene Mack had fallen into some kind of hole. A large, quite deep hole, he found as he struggled to extricate himself. It had been covered over by leaves and brush so that he had not seen it. He gritted his teeth in anger. At just the moment he had squeezed the trigger, a rotten branch that lay over this sink-hole or whatever it was had given way and plunged him to a depth above his knees into a damp and mucky morass of leaves and twigs.

And his shot had missed. He knew that.

Alice was amazed to find suddenly that Gus was at her side. Someone had fired a shot over her head, but it couldn't have been Gus. His hands were empty of any weapon. Nor had it been Frank Wells who fired, because if he had she wouldn't be standing here—she'd be doubled over with a gut wound.

Instinctively Frank shifted the angle at which he held the automatic, covering the new arrival.

"Frank, put that down," Gus ordered. "Drop it."

"Get back, Ferguson! You get back!" But it was Frank who backed up. Ferguson Brady didn't move.

"It's all over, Frank," Ferguson said. "Quit before anyone else gets hurt. You don't want—"

"You don't know what I want!" Only now did Frank become aware that someone had fired a shot. He had been so startled to see Ferguson unexpectedly materialize that he hadn't had time to wonder—

Or *had* he fired, himself? He was so upset now it was hard to remember what had just happened.

And he must waste no more time. He steadied the gun in his hand and fired.

As he pulled the trigger he knew, depressingly, that he was chickening out. He wasn't going to kill Ferguson, because he couldn't bring himself to take lethal aim. He liked him too well. At the last second he aimed away from the heart—at the right shoulder.

Disable him, and he could still get away—leave Connecticut and start a new life somewhere else, under another name.

The bullet knocked Gus backward against the boulder, and he was aware of a numbness in his arm. It felt as if he'd received a heavy-weight punch. But after only a moment he launched himself at Frank and brought him to the ground.

The gun dropped from Frank's fingers onto a beautiful little patch of moss and Alice picked it up, just as Officer John Tully, his revolver drawn, burst from the trees along the path coming up from the river and came panting up to them.

"I've got him covered, John." Gene Mack spoke from the top of the escarpment above, and they all looked up at him. "I'll take that," he told Alice and climbed down the twenty feet of rock face to relieve her of Frank Wells's automatic.

Gus, getting to his feet, found himself wrapped in Alice's arms. "Oh, darling, you've been shot!" Blood flowed down his arm and dripped to the ground.

"Here." Gene took a clean handkerchief from his pocket and handed it to Alice. "You can bandage him up with this." And to Ferguson, "It's not too bad, is it?"

He shook his head. "Flesh wound."

Frank stood with his head bent, looking at nothing. "You

214

can believe me or not," he said softly, "but if I'd intended to, I'd have killed you. I aimed to the side."

Ferguson nodded. "I believe you, Frank." He was looking not at Frank but at Alice, as she tied up the wound in his upper arm.

"Sorry my shot missed," Gene said, looking levelly at him. "Something gave way under my foot and spoiled my aim." Thank God no one could have noticed that he'd fired at the wrong man.

Ferguson Brady wasn't listening to him. He was aware only of Alice's fingers on his skin, her hair brushing against his cheek. The moment she knotted the handkerchief he took her in his arms.

"You okay to make it back to the road?" Gene asked as the two officers prepared to escort their prisoner up the rock escarpment and back to Gene's car, the shortest route out of the glen.

"Sure."

"We'll need you both at headquarters for an account of what happened."

"Yeh. We'll be there." And as the group receded out of earshot, "The poor bastard! Frank—of all people!"

The three of them disappeared over the highest rock ledge.

"Oh, Gus!" Alice breathed against his cheek.

He kissed her. The throbbing in his arm felt wonderful. He was a new man—Gus Brady, ten feet tall and able to slay dragons.

"We'll live at *my* house," he decided. "Okay?" He would never make the mistake his father had of moving into his bride's ancestral home. Alice was bossy enough as it was, and he would have to take a firm hand with her from the beginning.

"Poochie, too?" And he saw that the white spotted dog

215

had come out of the underbrush and was jumping up on Alice. "How did he get here, anyway?" She patted the furry head.

"He helped me search—he's a great tracker. But I guess he hid till all the trouble was over."

They started down the path.

He looked back on his life before today and shuddered. How could he have lived so long—for thirteen years it had been—in a state of arrested development? Only now had he been enabled to emerge from it as from a cocoon.

What if Alice had not come? He wondered whether he would have gone on into old age a withered pupa, never knowing of the adult stage he had failed to reach . . .

He touched her shoulder as she walked ahead of him, and she turned.

"I love you," he said, and was free at last of the nightmare chrysalis in which for so long he had been imprisoned.